Bello:
hidden talent rediscovered!

Bello is a digital only imprint of Pan Macmillan,
established to breathe new life into previously published,
classic books.

At Bello we believe in the timeless power of the imagination,
of good story, narrative and entertainment and we want to use
digital technology to ensure that many more readers
can enjoy these books into the future.

We publish in ebook and Print on Demand formats
to bring these wonderful books to new audiences.

About Bello:

www.panmacmillan.com/imprints/bello

About the author:

www.panmacmillan.com/author/paulsomers

Paul Somers

Paul Somers is the pen name of Paul Winterton (1908–2001). He was born in Leicester and educated at the Hulme Grammar School, Manchester and Purley County School, Surrey, after which he took a degree in Economics at London University. He was on the staff of *The Economist* for four years, and then worked for fourteen years for the *London News Chronicle* as reporter, leader writer and foreign correspondent. He was assigned to Moscow from 1942–5, where he was also the correspondent of the BBC's Overseas Service.

After the war he turned to full-time writing of detective and adventure novels and produced more than forty-five books. His work was serialized, televised, broadcast, filmed and translated into some twenty languages. He is noted for his varied and unusual backgrounds – which have included Russia, newspaper offices, the West Indies, ocean sailing, the Australian outback, politics, mountaineering and forestry – and for never repeating a plot.

Paul Somers was a founder member and first joint secretary of the Crime Writers' Association.

Paul Somers

THE
SHIVERING
MOUNTAIN

BELL◎

First published in 1959 by Collins

This edition published 2012 by Bello
an imprint of Pan Macmillan, a division of Macmillan Publishers Limited
Pan Macmillan, 20 New Wharf Road, London N1 9RR
Basingstoke and Oxford
Associated companies throughout the world

www.panmacmillan.com/imprints/bello
www.curtisbrown.co.uk

ISBN 978-1-4472-1591-2 EPUB
ISBN 978-1-4472-1590-5 POD

Visit **www.panmacmillan.com** to read more about all our books
and to buy them. You will also find features, author interviews and
news of any author events, and you can sign up for e-newsletters
so that you're always first to hear about our new releases.

Chapter One

The day the first hint of the Landon drama reached us at the *Record* was one of the quietest I'd ever known in Fleet Street. It was a Sunday—the thirteenth of March, to be exact. I was on the day-shift, and looking forward to the end of it. Blair, the News Editor, was more than usually on edge, having failed to find in the Sunday papers a single story worth following up. His ox-like shoulders were humped in worry over a mound of cuttings as he searched in vain for ideas. The only fresh news was of the most trivial kind. There'd been a report from Bromley that someone had taken a pot shot at a passing train and Smee had been sent to investigate. Mabel Learoyd had gone to Woking to interview a boy in hospital who was supposed to have hatched a raven's egg under his arm. The rest of us hadn't even made a telephone inquiry. At five o'clock, when Hatcher, the Night News Editor, took over from Blair, there was still nothing doing. The only difference was that whereas Blair merely fussed when there was no news about, Hatcher behaved like a maniac. He was a thin, grizzled man of fifty with a barrack-room manner and a conviction that News Was Made At Night and that he had a special gift for making it. Within five minutes he was barking orders all round the office—and it wasn't long before I got mine. He suddenly came rushing out of the News Room with a wild look in his eye bellowing, "Curtis . . .! Fire . . .! Temple . . .!" I walked round to the Temple and after a bit of trouble I managed to trace the alleged fire to somebody's chambers. The occupant had thrown a match into a waste-paper basket and the paper had caught alight and he'd put the fire out and that was that. I went back to the News Room and started to tell Hatcher

I

there was no story. He shouted, "Don't tell me about it—write it!" He was in a childish mood, even for him. I shrugged and went into the Reporters' Room and opened my typewriter.

Smee had just returned from Bromley and was tapping out the introduction to his story. He was a heavy, slow-moving man, with an air of being much put-upon. The previous day he'd been told to get more life into his stories, and judging by the sweat that was pouring off him he was giving this one all he had. The rest of the day staff were just fooling around—rather tactlessly, I thought, considering the atmosphere in the News Room. Fred Hunt, the Chief Reporter, and Ames, the Air Correspondent, were playing cricket with a paper ball and a broken chair leg. Parker, another reporter, had borrowed the coloured inks that Smee used for working out his complicated racing system, and was putting the finishing touches to what appeared to be an illuminated address. I went and had a look. It was a carefully penned quatrain set in a scroll of purple and green and it read:

"You cannot hope to bribe or twist,
Thank God, the British journalist,
But seeing what the man will do
Unbribed, there's no occasion to."

Parker said, "I like a bright room to work in, don't you? Where do you think's the best place to hang it?"

I grinned, and went back to my typewriter and wrote a sentence about the fire that never was and slipped the copy into Hatcher's in-tray while he was busy on the phone. After that there was peace of a kind, and I read a couple of book reviews in the *Observer*. Then Hatcher started shouting again and I looked up to see Smee emerging from the News Room with a homicidal look on his face. Ames said, "What's the trouble, Smee?" and deftly tweaked a piece of copy from his hand as he passed. He started to read it aloud. Smee had certainly got life into his story this time. The first line was: "Bang! Bang! Three shots rang out!"

There was a howl of laughter. Smee, looking injured, took the copy back. "Anyone can see I left the third 'bang' out by mistake," he said. "Anyone but that bastard . . .!"

"Must get your facts right, Smee!" Ames said. "Great national newspaper, you know—readers depend on us—Press Council watching."

"I'll do that bastard one of these days," Smee said, "you see if I don't. . . ." He went on his way, muttering.

I glanced at the clock. There was only a quarter of an hour to go till seven and then I'd be off duty. I'd no plans for the evening except to get away from Hatcher—but that was beginning to seem pretty important. I shut my desk and went along to wash. When I got back, Thomas, one of the office boys, was looking for me. "Mr. Hatcher says will you go out on this," he said, and gave me a grubby piece of paper with a message on it that he'd obviously taken down himself on the phone. It was from a porter at the Uxford Cross Hospital, who usually tipped us off if anyone interesting was brought in. This time it was something different. The message said that a Mrs. Ward had been called to the hospital by someone who'd phoned to tell her her father had been in a car smash and was asking for her, and when she'd got there she'd found it wasn't true. It was a nasty but commonplace sort of hoax—certainly not worth going out on.

I went into Hatcher, fuming.

"Well?" he snarled.

"I'm off at seven," I said.

"That's what you think! We're short-staffed tonight."

It was a thundering lie but I knew there was no point in arguing about that. I said, "This call was obviously made by someone with a kink."

"How do you know? Go and see the woman—you've got the address. Call in on your way home."

The address was Palmers Road, Maida Vale—nearly in Kilburn. Hatcher knew very well that I lived in Chancery Lane, a stone's throw from the office. He knew as well as I did that there'd be no story. He was being deliberately bloody-minded. I looked at Blair, who was still technically in charge and could have overruled him.

3

But Blair, his ears pink, was sorting his papers and pretending not to notice. I decided that with Hatcher in that mood it would be less wearing to go than to have a row. I collected my hat and coat, got my Riley from the office garage, and drove to Maida Vale.

Palmers Road was a street of terraced, two-storied, two-roomed houses that had gone up in the world since they were workmen's cottages, but not much. The district was a sort of poor man's Chelsea, with a few colour-washed walls and brightly painted front doors and window-boxes, and a lot of drabness in between. The night was overcast and very dark and I had to use a torch to find Mrs. Ward's number—forty-two. There was a small Ford car standing outside the house. The curtains were closely drawn across the downstairs window but a faint light showed through. At least Mrs. Ward was home again—which meant I shouldn't have to hang about. It looked as though she'd reported the hoax, because there was a police radio car parked a few yards away on the opposite side of the road. There were two men in it, watching me. As I approached the door, one of them left the car and crossed over to me. He was in plain clothes. "Good evening, sir," he said. "Do you want somebody at 42?"

I paused with my hand on the knocker. "Yes—Mrs. Ward."

"Ward?" The policeman gave me a searching look. "Who are you?"

"Hugh Curtis, of the *Record*," I told him.

He seemed surprised. "What's your business?"

I said, "We understand Mrs. Ward was called to the Uxford Cross Hospital this evening by a hoax message—something about her father having had an accident. When she got there she found it wasn't true. I'd like a couple of words with her, that's all. . . . Is there any objection?"

For a moment the policeman just stared at me. Then, to my astonishment, he turned and began to bang loudly on the door. No one came. There was no sound at all from inside. The second man got out of the radio car and started to come over. The plain clothes man suddenly said, "Lend a shoulder, will you?" and heaved his weight against the door. I added my twelve stone. At the second

4

combined heave the lock burst and the door flew open and I went in with the two men.

The entry had been so abrupt and dramatic that I wouldn't have been surprised at anything I'd found inside—even a body on the floor. In fact, the place seemed to be empty. The plain clothes man shouted "*Landon!*" in a voice rough with anxiety, bounded up the stairs to the bedroom and bathroom, rushed down again, and plunged into the bijou kitchen, switching on the light there. The kitchen was empty, too. It smelled strongly of onions. There was a crackle of broken glass under foot as the men moved to the back door, and I saw that a pane had been broken out jaggedly from the glazed top half of the door, just above the lock. On the floor there was a tell-tale mess of treacled brown paper and splintered glass. The door was closed, but not locked. The plain clothes man jerked it open and we shone our torches out. There was a tiny garden, the width of the house, with a six-foot brick wall round it and a solid wooden gate at the end, opening on to a narrow paved path that ran all along the back of the terrace. The wooden gate had been left ajar. I looked at the plain clothes man, and he was whiter than any cop I'd ever seen.

He turned and made for the radio car at the double. The uniformed policeman was poking about in the garden—looking, I imagined, for whatever had been used to smash the glass. I hadn't a clue what it was all about, but I thought I'd better look around while the going was good. Apart from the broken glass in the kitchen, there was no sign of any disturbance. The table in the sitting-room was laid for an evening meal for two. There was an assortment of delicatessen food, attractively arranged on a large plate. A bottle of cheap red wine stood in front of an electric fire, as though it had been put there to warm. The fire had been switched off. In the kitchen there was a half-chopped onion on the draining board, with a knife beside it, and some lettuce in a salad shaker. The kitchen looked pretty untidy, with several dirty saucepans and some crockery left over from lunch or breakfast. In one of the cupboards there were five empty gin bottles. I went upstairs and had a look in the bedroom. That was untidy, too, with clothes flung higgledy-piggledy over a chair back and face powder spilled on the dressing-table and several glossy magazines scattered around the floor. The clothes were good, and so was the furniture but the general air of the place was distinctly sluttish.

I got back to the sitting-room just as the plain clothes man came in from the car. He still looked like death, and if he felt any gratitude because I'd helped him break open the door he didn't show it. He just jerked his thumb towards the street and said "Out!" I started to ask him what was happening but he gave me a shove through the door and banged it behind me. I'd never been much good with policemen, but to-night looked like being an all-time low.

I was just debating whether to phone the office or stick around for a while when another police car arrived. Almost immediately afterwards a taxi drew up and a girl got out—a striking brunette, very pale. I caught no more than a glimpse of her, but there was something about her face that seemed vaguely familiar. Before I could get near her, the police had hustled her indoors.

It was very annoying. Something pretty unusual had happened, to judge by the fuss, and so far I had the story to myself. But I wouldn't have for long—and anyway, what *was* the story? I mentally went over what I knew, trying to piece the bits together. The householder, Mrs. Ward, had been expecting someone to dinner. Then she'd suddenly abandoned her preparations and gone out. That, presumably, had been when she'd got the bogus phone call about her father. In her absence, the house had been forcibly entered from the rear. That suggested that the bogus call had been made to get her out of the way. The police in the car had seemed to be watching the house when I arrived. They'd been quite unperturbed then. My story about the bogus call had been news to them—bad news. I'd had the impression they'd thought Mrs. Ward was still in the house. They'd certainly thought someone named "Landon" was in the house, and all hell had broken loose when they'd discovered he wasn't. I hadn't an inkling who Landon was, but he obviously mattered. It was all most intriguing, but so far it didn't make a lot of sense to me.

By now, of course, the neighbours had begun to take notice, and several doors stood open. A man was looking out of Number 43, next door to Mrs. Ward's, and I went to talk to him. At least the police couldn't stop me doing that. He was a greying, elderly man, with a forehead etched into quadrilaterals like the mud in a dried-up pond, and a very deep voice. He was as curious as I was about what was going on. I told him what I knew and then started to pump him about Mrs. Ward. The first thing I learned was that I'd got the name wrong—it was "Waugh," not "Ward," which no doubt accounted for the odd look I'd got from the policeman. Someone, probably Thomas, hadn't troubled to check the spelling. Mrs. Waugh was the brunette who'd just got out of the taxi. She was something in the theatrical world, the man said. There was no Mr. Waugh around—the girl was divorced, and lived alone. Her first name was Clara. Clara Waugh! Suddenly I thought I knew why her face had seemed familiar. I said, "Hasn't she been in the newspapers lately?" "That's right," the man said, "over the Angel murder—she and her fiancé heard the shots fired and called the police." This was interesting. Clara was obviously incident-prone. I asked the man if he remembered the fiancé's name, which I'd forgotten, and he said, yes, it was Ronald Barr. I asked him if the name "Landon" meant anything to him, and he said it didn't. I asked him if the Ford car belonged to Clara; and his wife, who'd joined him at the door, said "No," it belonged to a middle-aged man who'd visited Clara several times lately. They'd noticed him because on each occasion a police car had come with him. I assumed this must be Landon. They said he'd arrived that evening at about half-past six. They hadn't seen Clara go out, but now that I mentioned it they remembered hearing her telephone ringing at about six. I asked them if they'd heard any disturbance during the evening, any sound of breaking glass, but they hadn't.

I thanked them, and made a note of their name, which was Gregson, and moved round to the other side of 42. There was no one in at 41, but at 40 I had a bit more luck. A girl in bright green slacks and a yellow pullover said she'd understood the middle-aged man in the Ford was Clara Waugh's father—but she couldn't tell me anything much about him. I walked round the Ford and tried to take a look inside, but a policeman told me to move on. I made a note of the car's registration number and went off to phone the office. I dictated a cautious piece to a telephonist and afterwards I was put through to Hatcher on the Desk.

He said, "What do *you* want?" He was the rudest man I'd ever known. He seemed quite to have forgotten that he'd sent me out on a story. It was galling to have to admit that my unpromising errand had paid off, but there was no help for it, and I could sense his bad temper ebbing away as I talked. I said the police were around in shoals, and that I thought something pretty big was in the wind. I said Landon was obviously the key to the whole thing, and considering the surveillance and the police shut-down on news it looked as though there might be a security angle. I gave him the registration number of the Ford and suggested that Clara Waugh's fiancé might be able to tell us something about Landon if the office could get hold of him.

"We'll have a try," Hatcher said. "Excellent, Curtis—excellent. . . . By the way, aren't you off at seven?"

I said I had been!

"Right—hang on for a bit and I'll send someone to relieve you. Good night."

I walked back to Number 42. By now the road was stiff with official-looking cars, and more V.I.P.s were still arriving. A whale of a conference must be going on inside the house. There were several other reporters on the job now but I pretended to know as little as they did and kept out of their way.

About half-past eight a grey private car drew up near the house and a man got out. I heard him tell the sergeant on the door that he was Ronald Barr and that he'd been telephoned for, and he was allowed in. He looked pretty agitated.

Ten minutes later, Lawson arrived. Lawson was the *Record's* chief crime reporter. He was a slim, jaunty little man with a pallid face and an air of having come straight from the Tree of Knowledge. He was a bit disgruntled to-night—it seemed it was his day off and he'd been entertaining a new girl friend at his flat and Hatcher had rung him up at a rather critical moment—but he soon cheered up when I told him what had happened. At the mention of Clara Waugh's name he gave a low whistle, as though that altered everything. He'd been on the Angel murder case and obviously knew something about her but he didn't tell me what.

"Well, I'd better get cracking," he said, in a tone that suggested only a little effort was needed to clean up the whole story. I told him the police weren't being at all co-operative. "That's all right, old boy," he said, "just leave it to me." He moved with assurance towards the door of forty-two. I stood and watched. Lawson usually got on well with the police and I was always fascinated by his technique. He went confidently up to the sergeant and asked him if Superintendent Bailey was on the case, as though he and the superintendent were the closest of buddies. This time, though, it didn't work. There were a few brief exchanges, and then Lawson was told to stand back, and when he still hung around the sergeant got nasty and said something about "obstruction."

After a moment Lawson rejoined me. "Imagine promoting a chap like that!" he said. "Why, he's practically a half-wit."

I grinned. "Well, good luck, maestro!" I said. "I'm off."

I drove into Soho and had something to eat and then went back to the office to see if there'd been any developments. But almost nothing had happened. The whole night staff had been at work trying to get a line on Landon but there'd been nothing helpful in any of the personal files or reference books. He was still no more than a name. The Ford car had had a Buckinghamshire registration, but the ownership couldn't be established till next morning and perhaps not then if the police clamped down. Someone had been sent to the hospital to talk to the porter, but nothing fresh had emerged except that Mrs. Waugh had seemed just as worried after she'd learned the phone call was a hoax as before. Smee had just failed to catch Ronald Barr before he'd been called to Palmers Road. Lawson was still on the job. That was all.

I went up to the library to refresh my memory on the Angel case. As it turned out, Clara Waugh's part in it had been very small. On 11th February, which was just over a month ago, she'd been spending the evening with Barr at his flat in Saffron Mews,

Chelsea. The flat was one of four, with garages underneath. The couple had been having a few drinks and playing gramophone records. Between records they'd heard sounds of quarrelling in the flat next door, the end one, occupied by a man named Frank Angel. One of the voices had been a woman's. Then, while a record was playing, they'd heard what had sounded like shots. Barr had switched off, and after a moment they'd gone down to investigate. As they'd reached the mews a woman had rushed past them. Barr had started to go after her but she'd had a car waiting and she'd got away before he could stop her or get the number. Barr had rung Angel's door-bell and got no answer and he'd then gone back to his own flat and dialled 999. The police had arrived and forced Angel's door and found him lying dead on the floor of his sitting-room with two revolver bullets in him. Barr hadn't seen enough of the woman in the darkness to be able to describe her, and to Clara she'd been just a flying figure. In reply to questions at the inquest, Barr had said that he'd noticed several women going up to Angel's flat at different times, but he'd never liked being pried on himself and he'd deliberately not paid much attention. He'd been on good-neighbourly terms with Angel, and occasionally he and his fiancée had run into him at the local and they'd bought each other drinks and chatted and once at the pub he'd given Angel some advice about buying a car, but he hadn't been in his confidence at all and knew scarcely anything about him. He thought it most unlikely he'd be able to identify any of the women. That was really all about Barr and Clara. The police, however, *had* managed to identify one of the women, a wealthy middle-aged widow named Constance Albury, and she'd given some pretty meaty evidence. Under pressure she'd admitted that she'd been keeping Angel as her gigolo for more than a year. She'd been very fond of him, she said, and she'd visited him a number of times and he'd visited her quite often. She didn't know anything about any other women, but Frank had been such a handsome and fascinating man it wouldn't surprise her to know there'd been some.

I remembered Lawson's conclusion on the case—a

characteristically slanderous one, but quite possibly true. He'd told us, in his most confident, inside-information manner, that the police were pretty sure it was Mrs. Albury who'd killed Angel. Their view was that she *had* got to know about the other women, and that she'd called on him in jealous anger and quarrelled with him and shot him. According to her she'd been at her Hampstead home all the evening but she couldn't prove it—though, equally, the police couldn't prove she hadn't. No one had heard her leave home that evening, and the police hadn't been able to trace a revolver to her or indeed find any evidence that directly incriminated her. Both Barr and Clara had said they couldn't possibly tell whether the voice they'd heard through the wall was her voice. The weapon had never been found, so the police had had no help from fingerprints. The assumption was that Mrs. Albury had stuffed the gun into her handbag and got rid of it later. Anyway, there hadn't been enough evidence to bring a charge and the case had been shelved.

There was a certain amount of personal stuff in the cuttings and I looked through it all carefully. Clara was described as an actress, aged 25; Barr as a salesman, aged 33. There were pictures of both of them. The one of Clara was a studio photograph and showed her as a real beauty, with raven-black hair and sultry dark eyes and a full, attractively-shaped mouth. Barr had a strong, rather rugged face, with a square cleft chin. They made a fine-looking pair. Mrs. Albury had been photographed in the street at an unfortunate angle that gave her a sharp-featured and rather unpleasant look. Angel, I saw, had been strikingly handsome, in a debonair, film-star sort of way. He, also, had been 33. He was described as a dress designer—though the evidence at the inquest had made it pretty clear his only successful designs had been on Mrs. Albury.

I sat for a moment or two with the cuttings spread out in front of me, thinking about the case. It would be absurd, I told myself, to look for any connection between the Angel shooting and the Palmers Road affair. It wasn't as though Clara had played any important part in the Angel case. She'd heard the shots, that was all. It could have happened to anyone. It was almost certainly pure coincidence that she'd been caught up in this fresh trouble so soon afterwards—whatever the trouble might turn out to be. . . . All the same, I couldn't help wondering.

Chapter Two

I was on duty at eleven again next morning. I reported to Blair, who as usual was almost buried in a sea of papers. He greeted me most amiably. Thanks to my early arrival at Palmers Road the night before, we'd had a much fuller and more coherent story than any of our competitors, and though I'd done no more than a routine job I was temporarily the blue-eyed boy. I asked Blair if there'd been any developments and he said there hadn't. Clara Waugh's house had been besieged by newspapermen all night, but there'd been no statement from anyone. Ronald Barr had left for his own home at one in the morning, with a police escort to keep reporters away from him. A police car had remained on guard in Palmers Road. Lawson had hung on hopefully until four, and was now catching up on his sleep. The agencies had been prevented from finding out the address of the Ford car's owner by a police "stop" on all information from the registration office.

It was a complete shut-down, and for once even Blair seemed flummoxed about the next step. Then, at five-past eleven, the picture suddenly changed. The telephone rang on the News Desk. I saw Blair frowning over the receiver. A brief, excited exchange followed with Martin, the Assistant News Editor. Then Blair came bustling into the Reporters' Room, flushed with tidings. "Curtis," he said, "will you get right along to the Ministry of Supply? They're holding a Press conference there at 11.30 on the Palmers Road affair."

So it *was* a security matter. I dashed down to the Riley and stepped on the gas and reached the Ministry on the stroke of eleven-thirty. There was already a big crowd of reporters assembled in the waiting-room, but no sign of officialdom, yet I strolled out into the corridor again. A girl was just approaching from the lobby. With a glow of pleasure I saw that it was Mollie Bourne.

Mollie was the star reporter of our greatest rival, the *Courier*. She was so bright she was almost a galaxy. She enjoyed a very special reputation in Fleet Street, because she had a way of involving herself personally in big stories and then somehow getting into the news instead of just reporting it. I had particular reason to know it, because on more than one occasion she'd involved me too, with highly dramatic consequences for both of us. She was a girl who went all out on hunches—so much so that "Keep your eye on Mollie!" had become a kind of slogan at the *Record*. I admired her enormously, but my interest wasn't just professional. She was the most devastatingly attractive girl I'd ever met. She had rich chestnut hair—a wonderful colour—and dark, vivacious eyes, and a figure as satisfying as her looks. We were on fairly close terms, as a result of our adventurous encounters, but I'd have liked them to be much closer. In fact, it was my intention to marry her if I could ever prise her away from her job. I didn't think she was altogether against the idea as a long-term project, but she was very elusive and not at all to be taken for granted.

She said, "Hallo, Hugh!" and gave me a charming smile. As always, she was immensely self-possessed and exquisitely groomed. She was wearing a sage green suit and a hat so slight that it had probably cost her the earth. On three thousand a year and expenses she could afford it.

I said, "And how's the *Courier's* spoiled darling this morning?"

"Fine, thank you."

"I've been trying to get hold of you for nearly a week. . . . Where have you been hiding out?"

"Oh, here and there . . . I've been out of town a lot."

"I haven't seen any big scoops in the *Courier* lately."

"There hasn't been much to scoop, has there?"

I grinned. "Our Mr. Hatcher says a good reporter can always find a story."

"Hatcher! He doesn't know the difference between a story and a loud bang!"

"All the same, I suspect you're losing your touch. . . . I think it's time you retired on your laurels and got married."

"I don't want to retire."

"Then just get married. I wouldn't insist on your leaving the *Courier* right away."

"That's big of you."

"Not at all—I'm easy-going."

"I can't think of anything that would be more disastrous."

"What would be disastrous about it?"

"Everything, I should think. You'd always be pinching my by-lines, for one thing."

"If I did you could get a divorce—I'm sure that would rate as cruelty!"

"Besides, you'd be bound to be on the night turn when I was on the day turn."

"At least we could have fun when we met on the stairs."

"How very uncomfortable!"

"Well," I said, "you'd better watch out. You're twenty-four—you may find yourself on the shelf if you're not careful."

She smiled. "I dare say someone would reach up for me!"

"Anyway," I said, "what do you make of this story?"

"It looks rather promising, doesn't it?"

"*You* weren't in Palmers Road last night . . .?"

"Good heavens, no—I'm not a menial!"

The badinage ended there. Someone called out that we could go in now, and we all trooped into the Board Room. We were greeted by the Ministry's Public Relations Officer, a former newspaperman named Robson. He was a genial, pipe-smoking man, very friendly and discreet. He waved us to seats round the enormous green baize table. There were several people sitting there already, some of whom we knew and some of whom Robson introduced. One of them was Inspector John Darwin, of the Special Branch. Another was Superintendent Bailey, of the Yard—the policeman Lawson purported to be on confidential terms with. There were also several permanent officials of the Ministry. Clara Waugh was there, sitting on Robson's right, and beside her, Ronald Barr—presumably to give her moral support. I studied Clara with interest. At close quarters her looks weren't quite up to the photograph I'd seen—she was too heavily made up and her skin looked a bit coarse for twenty-five—but the bones of her face were lovely. Probably it wasn't fair to judge her to-day, when she was worried and short of sleep. Barr, I noticed, kept regarding her anxiously. With his broad shoulders and square chin he looked very solid and dependable.

Robson tapped out his pipe and cleared his throat. "Well, ladies and gentlemen, let me tell you right away what this is about.... Last evening, as most of you know, Mrs. Waugh's father, Arthur Landon, disappeared from her house in Palmers Road.... After all the secrecy there's been, you probably won't be surprised to hear that Mr. Landon is a physicist employed at the Ministry's Research Establishment at Crede in Buckinghamshire."

He was right—we weren't surprised. Something of the kind had been signalled all along. No one looked terribly excited at the news, either. It might turn out to be a wonderful story, but disappearing physicists were no longer the novelty they'd once been.

Robson proceeded to summarise the facts—most of which were already known to us. On the previous day, Landon had been going to have dinner with his daughter at her home. He had left the Crede Establishment at 5.35 p.m., driving his own Ford car. He had been accompanied, as a routine measure, by security officers whose job it was to take care of him. The two cars had reached the house in Palmers Road just after half-past six. A light had been on in the downstairs room and it had been assumed that Mrs. Waugh was there. In fact she had been called away at 6 p.m. by a bogus telephone message about an accident to her father. The security officers, having no notion of this, had stayed parked a few yards from the house, keeping watch. Landon had let himself in with his own key and closed the door behind him, and that was the last that had been seen of him. As a result of information brought by a reporter, the police had broken in at 7.20 p.m. and discovered that the house was empty. A smashed pane of glass in the back door showed that someone had entered during Mrs. Waugh's absence.

Robson paused for a moment. Then he went on: "What actually happened in the house is still a matter of guesswork, but it seems very likely that the intruder was waiting there when Landon arrived and that he forced him to leave at once by the back way. There were no signs of any struggle or injury in the house, so the supposition is that the intruder had a gun and that he compelled Landon to leave by threatening him with it. It would have been quite possible, of course, to march him in the dark to a waiting car at the end of the path that runs behind the terrace. However, as I say that's all speculation. The police, under Superintendent Bailey, have been over the whole place, but so far they've found nothing to help them. The door knobs, both inside and outside the back door, and also the door key, had been wiped clean of fingerprints, and no useful prints were discovered in the house. The night was dry, and there were no footmarks inside or outside. No witnesses have yet been discovered who heard or saw anything unusual. The whole affair was obviously planned and executed with great skill and precision. We have no idea what has happened to Landon, and we need the maximum co-operation of the Press in seeking information from the public. That's why it was decided to take the rather unusual step of holding this—er—informal conference, with everyone concerned present. In return for your co-operation, I need hardly say that the Ministry and the police will give you all the help in their power. Before we go any further perhaps you'd like to see the stuff we've prepared on Landon...."

Robson broke off, and there was a buzz of talk while photographs and a full description of the missing man were circulated. The only physicists I'd had anything to do with had all been plump, jolly men who could equally have been shopkeepers or publicans from their appearance, but Landon actually looked like the popular idea of an egghead. He had deep-set eyes, hollow cheeks, a long fine nose, and a thin mouth, so that the general impression was of an ascetic and rather intense man. But none of his features was exaggerated to the point where the face would attract immediate attention or its details linger in the mind. Indeed, the most conspicuous thing about him was a pair of very heavy, dark-rimmed glasses, which we gathered he always wore. I could see no resemblance whatever to Clara. The description said he was 49, had light-brown hair, greying slightly at the temples and sides, was 5 feet 11 inches tall, and lean but muscular. When last seen he had been wearing a dark grey suit, a black overcoat, a soft grey felt hat, black shoes, a white shirt, and a blue-and-grey striped tie. It was the sort of description that would have fitted thousands of professional men.

When we'd glanced through the stuff, Robson called us to order and said, "Well, now you can fire your questions. . . ."

There were a lot of questions, put by a lot of different reporters. I give them here, just as I took them down, with the answers and the brief comments I made at the time.

To P.R.O.

—Exactly how important was Landon's work?

—He was engaged on top secret work. All such work is obviously important. I understand the Minister is making a statement in the House this afternoon and I can't anticipate what he'll say. But I think I can tell you that Landon's loss would be a great one. (A nod from Ministry official.)

—Would it endanger our security?

—I certainly wouldn't say that—but I'd prefer to say nothing more on that at all.

—Are physicists at Crede always accompanied by security officers?

—Not always.

—So Landon was something special?

—As I say, his loss would be a great one.

—Do the Ministry think that whoever kidnapped him wanted to

make use of his knowledge—or just to put him out of action, so to speak?
—There's no evidence on that, either way.

—Is it thought he may still be alive? (Brutal—Barr puts hand on Clara's arm.)
—All I can say is, we hope so.

—Is it possible he's been taken out of the country?
—It seems unlikely. Certainly not by any normal route.

—Did Landon actually live at the Crede Establishment?
—Yes—he had a prefab there. There's quite a little community.

—Is he married?
—No, he's a widower.

To Clara

(Who's fiddling nervously with her engagement ring)
—Can you tell us anything, Mrs. Waugh, about the voice of the person who made the bogus telephone call to you?
—It was a man with a very deep, gruff voice.

—Did it sound like a natural voice?
—Well, it didn't strike me at the time that it wasn't, but I think now that it might have been put on. It's difficult to say.

—Did it sound foreign?
—Oh, no, not a bit.

—Was it the voice of an educated man, would you say?
—Yes.

—It didn't remind you of anyone you knew?
—No.

—What exactly did the man say?

—As far as I can remember, he said, 'Mrs. Waugh?—it's the police here. I'm sorry to tell you your father has had a car accident. There's no need for undue alarm—he's not in immediate danger. But he's asking for you. Could you come at once, please, to Uxford Cross Hospital?' I can't swear to the exact words, but that's more or less what he said.

To P.R.O.

—Who knew that Landon was going to visit Mrs. Waugh yesterday evening?

—That's an extremely important point, of course, and we're going into it very thoroughly. As far as we know at the moment—Mrs. Waugh herself; Mr. Barr; a friend of Mrs. Waugh's named Mrs. Elsie Morton, who rang up in the afternoon to see if Mrs. Waugh could look in for a drink in the evening and was told, no, because her father was coming; a next-door neighbour, named Miss Bright, at number 41, whom Mrs. Waugh had a talk with in the morning when she was getting the milk in; and a salesman at a local grocer's, where Mrs. Waugh bought a bottle of wine on Saturday. You can have the various addresses if you want them, but I may say that all these people have been carefully checked, without any helpful result. Landon himself told his Chief at the Establishment, Sir Maurice Proude, that he was going to see his daughter that evening, and he also mentioned it to two of his colleagues there, whose names at the moment we prefer not to give you for security reasons. Those are the people we know about. What we don't know, of course, is whether Landon mentioned the visit to anyone else.

—Could he have mentioned it to anyone outside the Establishment—without the security people knowing about it?

—Oh, certainly—he wasn't a prisoner, you know! And it wasn't their job to eavesdrop on his conversations—they were protecting him, that's all.

—*They* knew he was going to pay the visit, of course?
—The police ...? (Surprise) Well, yes ... Just before Landon left, I believe.... Anyhow, the whole question of who knew about the visit is still being looked into.

To Clara

—Did your father visit you at regular intervals, Mrs. Waugh?
—No, just any time.

—There was no routine that a kidnapper could have relied on?
—No routine at all. He'd been up several times lately—three week-ends running, in fact—tout before that I hadn't seen him for—oh, a month or two, I suppose.

—Was there any special reason for his coming three weeks running—anything that a kidnapper could have known about?
—Well, there *were* special things I wanted to discuss with him, but no one else could have known. I was a bit upset about the murder that happened next door to Mr. Barr—I expect you know about that—and I wanted to talk to him about it. Also, I'd just decided to become officially engaged to Ronald and Father hadn't met him, so of course that was another thing.

—When was this last visit actually decided on?
—The previous week-end. Father had seen Ronald, and they'd got on well, but of course I wanted to find out privately what he really thought, so I asked him up for a tête-à-tête. (Barr slightly sheepish.)

To P.R.O.

—Wouldn't it have been a good idea to take the Press into your confidence last night and circulate this description straight away, instead of sitting on the story and losing twelve hours?
   (Uncomfortably) "You'll appreciate that the disappearance of Landon raised matters of high policy, and by the time the necessary consultations had taken place it was too late to get anything in

the morning papers, or even on TV. We've moved as quickly as was practicable.

To *Inspector Darwin*

—Are you satisfied with the security job your men did?

(Also uncomfortably) "They could hardly have done more. We don't sit in people's pockets. We knew Landon was visiting his daughter, we saw him right into the house where we had every reason to believe she was. The same thing had happened on the two preceding week-ends, and all had been well. Besides, there was no reason at all to expect anything to happen. Landon was what is usually known as a 'back-room boy'—very few people could have realised his importance.

—All the same, Inspector, isn't it customary when you're watching premises to take a look round the back?

—One of my men did take a look round the back while he was waiting—he walked right down the path. But by then, of course, it was all over and the place was quiet.

To *P.R.O.*

—This is just a thought, and I don't suppose it has any bearing on the case at all—but I suppose Landon was considered a good security risk?

—The best possible. He had a first-class record in every way. He wasn't concerned with politics, and as far as we know he had no worries, no difficulties of any sort.

—No relatives behind the Iron Curtain? No possibility of any pressure on him?

—Nothing like that at all.

—What about his health?

—(Pause.) Well, I'll be absolutely frank with you—he *had* complained to his chief recently about excessive tiredness. He's been working at very high pressure and it showed a little. But it was nothing at all serious—nothing that a short holiday wouldn't put right.

To Clara

—Just one or two points of detail, Mrs. Waugh. I assume you locked the back door before you went out?

—I must have done, or the intruder wouldn't have had to break in—but I don't actually remember. I usually do, so I expect I did it from force of habit.

—Did you switch off the electric fire?

—Yes, I do remember doing that.

—Did the intruder turn the light on in the sitting-room, or did you leave it on?

—Apparently I left it on. I didn't know I had, but the people across the way say it was on all the time. I was so upset when I got that phone call I hardly knew what I was doing.

—We all understand that—and if I may say so we all sympathise. . . . There's just one other point, I couldn't quite understand how your father came to have a key to your house, as he wasn't a very frequent visitor.

—Oh, ages ago he used to stay at the house for a night occasionally when I was away, so he had to have a key. And as I'd got another one, he kept his.

To Supt. Bailey

—Wiping the door handles and key suggests that the intruder, whoever he was, thought he might be traced fairly easily through his fingerprints. Do you agree?

—It's certainly a point.

—We talk of the intruder, but there could, I suppose, have been more than one of them?

—There could well have been.

That was about all, and soon afterwards the conference broke up. Robson looked thankful it was over—I had the feeling it should really have been a Ministerial occasion, and that he'd been asked to handle it with the idea of playing down the disappearance and not causing too much alarm and despondency. It certainly had been a most unusual conference—I'd never known the security people expose themselves to reporters' fire before. It was just as though everyone was hurrying to be as frank as possible, getting in their explanations and trying to win over the Press before the public storm broke over them. I wondered exactly what work Landon *had* been doing.

For a few moments Clara continued to talk to a group of reporters, while Barr stood protectively by. She looked as though she'd be glad to get away, but the Press hadn't finished with her yet—she and Barr still had to pose for the photographers outside. I followed them into the street. Mollie's elegant cream-and-sage Sunbeam Talbot was parked at the kerb and she was standing beside it. I strolled up to her.

"What do you make of it all?" I said.

"It seems fairly straightforward."

"Except that we don't know where Landon is or who kidnapped him or why!"

"Well, I expect we shall in time...." Her mind didn't seem to be properly on the subject. I followed the direction of her gaze, and she was looking at Ronald Barr. "Don't you think Clara's fiancé is extraordinarily good looking?"

"I've seen worse."

"Those shoulders!—now there's something a girl could really lean her head on."

"Come and have a drink," I said. "I'd like to lean on a dry Martini."

"Sorry—I've got a lunch date ... I must fly."

"Dinner to-night, then."

"Not to-night, Hugh—some other time. I'll ring you."

"Is that a promise?"

"Yes...."

There was a bit of flurry behind me and I looked round. It was a messenger from the Ministry, sent to ask Clara if she'd mind going back for a moment to see Superintendent Bailey. Clara said, "Yes—all right." Barr was holding the door of his car. He said, "Well, darling, if I'm going to see Forbes I'd better be getting along. Try not to worry too much. I'll expect you around six." He bent to kiss her.

I turned again to Mollie, still hoping to make a firm date with her. She was staring at the couple as though she'd suddenly seen a ghost. I looked too, but I couldn't see any ghost.

I said, "What's the matter? Something struck you?"

"Yes," she said.

"Something interesting?"

She gave me a slightly preoccupied smile. "Perhaps you'd like a carbon copy of my story?" she said.

I phoned the News Desk, and had lunch, and then went back to the office to write up my notes. On the way in I passed Lawson coming out. He called "Hi!" but didn't stop. I took the lift up to the Reporters' Room, which was empty. Martin was holding the fort in the News Room. I stuck my head in.

"What's happened to the staff?" I asked.

"Blair's sent them all off to interview the people who knew about Landon visiting his daughter."

"Ah, yes. . . . Have the agencies sent much out?"

"Reams! You'd better have it."

I took the pile of copy from him. "What's Lawson doing around at this hour? He's not supposed to be on till five."

"I don't think he could keep away," Martin said, with a grin. "He says Landon's disappearance is a Crime and that he's the Crime Reporter. He was being very snooty about what he called Ministry 'hand-outs.' "

"What's *he* planning to do about it—start a one-man search?"

"I'm not sure. He read all the copy very carefully, and went into a huddle with Blair, and then he pushed off, looking mysterious. . . . I've an idea he's gone to see Superintendent Bailey."

"Really? I doubt if he'll get anything fresh out of him—Bailey didn't seem to know anything this morning."

"Well, we'll need a follow-up of some sort," Martin said. "This conference stuff's going to look pretty stale by the time the evenings have finished with it."

I nodded, and drifted back into the Reporters' Room, and settled down to write my piece.

The afternoon passed quietly. The only bit of fresh news was the Minister's statement in the House, and that didn't carry things much further. The gist of it was that Landon had been working on a special project of great importance to the defence programme and that his kidnapping could cause a setback, but that it would be an exaggeration to say the country's safety had been imperilled. After the statement there'd been some probing questions about the nature of the project, and the adequacy of the security precautions, and the steps that were being taken to trace Landon, but the Minister had sidestepped most of them on the usual ground that further information would be against the public interest. The police, he'd said, were "prosecuting their inquiries with the utmost vigour," and the House would be kept informed of any developments. There, for the moment, the matter rested.

Around four, the day staff began to trickle back from their respective missions. None of them had anything significant to report. The checks on Clara's neighbours and friends and tradesmen had produced nothing. Parker, who had been sent to Crede, hadn't been allowed inside the Establishment, which was hardly surprising. In the absence of hard news, we sat around and speculated. The general view seemed to be that Landon had been nabbed by foreign agents and quietly bumped off and that before long we'd hear that his body had been found in a ditch. But the view wasn't unanimous. Hunt thought that if agents had been going to kill him they'd have stuck a knife in his ribs in the back garden and not marched him off along a public path—always supposing that that was what had happened. "If you ask me," he said unexpectedly, "it's more likely that Landon's just done a bunk—gone over to the Russians, like the rest of them."

26

On the evidence, that seemed impossible. I said, "But it just doesn't stand up, Fred. What about the phone message calling Clara Waugh away?"

"That could have been fixed. If Landon had wanted to go over, he'd have *had* to fix up something pretty tricky, because he had the security chaps on his tail the whole time. He could have got an accomplice to make the phone call—some Russian with a good English accent—and then walked in through the front door and straight out through the back to a waiting car."

"What about the broken pane of glass? You're not suggesting he took a lump of treacled paper with him from Crede and broke the pane himself!"

"No, but his accomplice could have done that while Clara Waugh was out of the house. Easily."

"Well, it's possible," I agreed, "but it's not very likely. The security people seemed quite sure he was reliable."

"They admitted his health hadn't been good. Probably things had been preying on his mind.... Anyway, how often are the security people right?"

Parker said, "What would the Russians want Landon for, Fred—to teach them how to launch a sputnik? That's a laugh."

"I dare say we still know a few things they don't," Hunt said. "You'll see—there'll probably be pictures of him at the Bolshoi before the end of the week!"

Chapter Three

We didn't get a follow-up after all—but neither did anyone else. The nearest thing to a scoop next morning was a profile of Landon in the *Gazette*, contributed by an anonymous friend. It presented him as a patient, determined and self-absorbed scientist; a man of naturally warm feelings who had more and more withdrawn into his laboratory shell after the death of his wife; a man of great physical courage and endurance (a point illustrated by a mountaineering incident of his youth); and a man who—like most great scientists—could sometimes seem both eccentric and naïve to his friends. It was an interesting article and it threw quite a bit of light on Landon—but none, of course, on what had happened to him.

Apart from that, all the papers carried the same rather stale facts, written up in different ways. I read through Mollie's piece with particular care—I always did, when we were working on the same story—but like everyone else she'd only re-hashed the conference. Whatever it was she'd noticed outside the Ministry, it hadn't been significant enough to give her a new angle.

The case seemed to be completely in the doldrums when I reported to Blair just before eleven. I gathered that fifteen people had rung up the office from widely-scattered parts of the country to say they thought they'd seen a man answering to Landon's description, but according to Martin they'd all sounded vague or crazy and we were leaving it to the police to investigate them. Otherwise there was nothing.

The only man in the Reporters' Room was Lawson, who, according to the Duty List, should have been having another day off. He was typing away with an air of tremendous concentration. I'd never known him start work so early. I strolled over to his desk.

"Expenses?" I said.

"A memo, old boy." He took a cigarette from a packet and lit it with a quick flick of his lighter as though he hadn't a moment to lose. "For the Editor."

"Big stuff, eh?"

"Well, between you and me and the gatepost, old boy, I think I'm on the way to breaking this case wide open."

"You mean the Landon case?"

"Of course . . . I've been doing a lot of work on it since yesterday. Real work—not going to conferences. What's more, I've been doing some *thinking*." He spoke as though it were some rare ordeal he'd subjected himself to. "And I've got a theory."

I said, "I'd like to hear it."

"You'll keep it under your hat?"

"If it's anything like your usual theories," I said, "it'll be the only safe place for it!"

He ignored that. "Well, the fact is I don't accept that Ministry stuff at all—not any part of it. I think they've got hold of the wrong end of the stick entirely. Just because Landon was a physicist they've taken it for granted that that's why he was kidnapped. I don't believe it. I don't believe he could possibly have been abducted by some kind of enemy agent."

"Why do you say that?"

"Because of the evidence, old boy. Whoever pulled this job knew pretty well everything there was to know about Landon and Clara Waugh and the set-up at Palmers Road. He knew Landon was going to visit his daughter that evening. He knew there was an approach to Clara's house from the back. He knew the garden gate wouldn't be locked. He probably knew there was a high wall round the garden or he couldn't have taken the risk of breaking in. He knew Clara was alone in the place. He knew Landon would let himself in with his own key. He knew the police would stay quietly outside and let Landon go in alone. He knew the time Landon was going to arrive to within a few minutes—he must have been able to bank on that, because if Landon had turned up a quarter of an hour earlier it wouldn't have been properly dark and the intruder wouldn't have been able to march him out. Those are just a few of the things. For my money, they don't add up to an enemy agent—they add up to someone with very intimate knowledge of the family."

I was silent for a moment. Then I said, "Surely an agent could have had intimate knowledge. He'd have needed the right contacts, of course, but that would be part of his job—to get them. For all we know there may be someone planted right inside the Crede Establishment. Perhaps a close colleague of Landon's—one of the chaps who was told he was going to visit his daughter. As for the rest of the information, a good agent would naturally reconnoitre the place pretty thoroughly beforehand. He could have pretended to be a tradesman or something. And he could easily have been around during one of Landon's previous visits, and seen that Landon used his own key and that the police waited outside. . . . Well, perhaps not easily, with the police watching, but I'm sure he could have managed it somehow. He might even have fixed himself up in one of the neighbouring houses. . . ." I paused. "Anyway, if Landon wasn't abducted because he was a physicist, why *was* he abducted?"

"Ah!" Lawson hitched his chair a little closer to mine and dropped his voice, though there was no one else in the room. "Now that's just it. That's where I think the Ministry hasn't been able to see the wood for the trees. . . . My idea, old boy, is that someone had a jolly good reason for getting rid of Landon, a personal reason, and used the fact that he was a valued scientist as a kind of cover. That would be a pretty clever plan, wouldn't it? Setting the whole country off on a spy hunt, when the truth was close at home!"

"But *did* anyone have a good reason for getting rid of Landon, apart from the public one?"

"The answer to that is, yes, old boy. I told you I'd been doing a bit of sleuthing. Yesterday evening I had a long private chat with Bailey. I asked him if he'd had a look into Landon's private life at all—personal, financial, that sort of thing. He had, of course—just part of the routine. And do you know what I found out? Landon had a big die-to-win insurance policy with the Star and General . . . Ten thousand pounds."

"Really?"

"It's a fact. Apparently he used to do a good deal of rock-climbing when he was a young man and he took the policy out soon after his daughter was born, as a protection for his wife, and kept it going from habit. So now, assuming he's dead, somebody inherits ten thousand pounds, which is quite a lot of lolly. And I'll give you one guess who inherits."

"His daughter, I suppose."

"You're absolutely right. His daughter—and indirectly, of course, her fiancé, Mr. Barr. And there's your motive! Get the idea? My theory, old boy, is that Clara and Barr conspired together to get rid of the old man and cash in. Clara made the arrangements for her father's visit, including roughly the time he'd arrive. Barr made the bogus telephone call—just so the neighbours could hear the phone ring. Clara went off to the hospital, having broken the pane of glass in the back door earlier in the day to make it look as though a stranger had got in during her absence. Barr parked his car at the end of the path and sneaked into the house by the back way and waited inside for Landon. As soon as Landon came in he stuck a gun in his back, marched him to the car, bashed him on the head with a spanner, and dumped the body in a quiet spot. And now Barr and Clara are both sitting pretty. . . . Well, what do you think of it?"

I was speechless. Lawson's theories usually carved swathes through people's reputations without much regard for evidence, but this one went far beyond anything I'd heard yet. I said, "I think it's the lousiest, most unlikely theory you've ever put up. . . . Is this what you've been so busy typing?"

"More or less."

"Then if you take my advice you'll tear it up before anyone sees it. Otherwise they'll get you for criminal libel before you can say Old Bailey."

Lawson looked quite unabashed. "Why do you say it's unlikely?"

"What—*parricide?*"

"Be your age, old boy—it's happened often enough. What about Lizzie Borden? You don't want to let yourself be taken in by these women, you know—you can't trust any of 'em. Particularly the good-lookers. And *I'd* say Clara Waugh's just the type. I found out a few things about her at the time of the Angel case—I've made quite a study of her. *I've* been doing some real investigating—not just sitting on my backside at a green baize table! Her mother was Italian—did you know that? Real Borgia blood there! Dark passion and all that. You may think she seems quite normal, but she's not all she appears to be—not by a long chalk. She tried to give the impression she was fond of her father, didn't she?—but I can tell you it's all my eye. . . ." He glanced round the room to make sure we were still alone. "Here, take a look at this. . . ."

He thrust a sheet of notepaper into my hand. It was a brief letter, written from the Crede Establishment and dated about two months back. It said:

DEAR CLARA,

I was very distressed by the tone of your letter. I wrote as I did the other day only because I'm very fond of you and thought it was my duty—not because I want to interfere in your life. I wish you'd let me come and see you, so that we could talk about things. It's nearly eight months since we met, and that's far too long.

Your affectionate Father,
ARTHUR LANDON

I said, "Where on earth did you get this from?"

Lawson grinned. "From Clara's house. I heard she was spending yesterday evening with her fiancé at his place, so I went along to Palmers Road to see what I could find out. The cops had gone, so I popped in and had a look round."

"One of these days," I said, "you'll be jailed for breaking and entering—and it'll serve you damned well right!"

"Not breaking, old boy, not this time—just entering. The smashed pane hasn't been mended yet—and with those high walls round, it seemed too good a chance to miss. . . . Anyway, what do you make of the letter?"

"Well," I said cautiously, "it's obvious they'd been having a bit of a row—but it's equally obvious that Clara responded to his letter and that they patched things up all right. Landon's certainly been seeing a lot of her lately."

"That doesn't mean a thing—it could have been part of the plot. Clara would naturally have had to invite him along once or twice if she and Barr were planning to bump him off. They'd have wanted to get him used to the routine."

"She could just as well have wanted him to get to know her fiancé, as she said."

"She could, old boy, but I don't think she did. My guess is that it was a sort of rehearsal. I think they wanted to make sure the police got used to staying outside when he arrived, and that he got used to letting himself in. . . . Why do you suppose he'd been given his own key?"

"Clara explained that. He used the place when she was away, and hung on to the key afterwards."

"That's what she said, but is it likely? Why would a man in Landon's position go to a dump like Palmers Road and stay there on his own when he could have gone to a decent hotel? I can tell you this—none of the neighbours *remember* him staying there alone, because I checked."

"They probably wouldn't remember anyway, if it was just the odd night. Besides, Clara said it was some time ago."

"Well, I don't believe he was ever there alone. I don't believe he had a key until recently. I think Clara gave him the key because she knew that on the fatal night she wouldn't be at home, she'd be at the hospital, so he'd *have* to let himself in. It sticks out a mile."

"Not to me," I said. "It can't be all that unusual for a father to have a key to his daughter's house."

"I'd say it was pretty unusual, if the father's a rare visitor and

33

not on very good terms with his daughter. . . . Anyway, while we're on this question of visits, there's another thing. Clara must have something on her conscience, or she'd have been more frank. At that so-called news conference you attended, she said she hadn't seen her father, until these last few visits, for 'a month or two.' Those were her actual words. Now would *you* say eight months was 'a month or two'? 'A few months,' maybe, but not 'a month or two.' "

"She was in a pretty worried state when she said that, Lawson."

"I don't believe she could have made that mistake just out of worry—I'd say the statement was a deliberate lie. Obviously she wouldn't want to give the impression she'd been on strained terms with the old man if she'd just helped to bump him off."

"Then why did she leave this letter lying about for anyone to find?"

"It was with a lot of others—she probably overlooked it. Murderers always overlook something, you know that. . . . Anyway, I've not finished yet, not by a long way. Tell me this! Why was the light on in the downstairs room?"

"Clara said she forgot to turn it off. It seems reasonable enough, considering the state she was in."

"She remembered to lock the back door and turn the electric fire out, so why should she forget to turn the light off . . .? But that's not really the point I'm trying to make. What I want to know is, *why was the light ever on?* Look, old boy, she left her house sharp at six o'clock, directly she got the bogus call. Lighting-up time that evening was six thirty-one. What was she doing with a light on in the sitting-room before six?"

"It was an exceptionally dark night," I said.

Lawson shook his head. "I don't think that was the reason at all. I think she *had* to leave the light on, because if the house had been in darkness when Landon arrived the police would have realised she wasn't at home and might have started wondering. As it was, no one suspected anything."

"She could have arranged for Barr to turn the light on when he arrived. That would have done just as well."

"What, and have those people opposite notice that the light had come on while she was out! That would have been far too risky. . . . It's no use, old boy, everything fits. Even the fact that there weren't any fingerprints on the door-knobs and key. An unknown enemy agent wouldn't have needed to worry about leaving his fingerprints—but Barr and Clara would. And they knew it. They're clever, those two!"

I wasn't impressed. "What you're doing," I said, "is deliberately giving a sinister explanation to a lot of quite innocent facts. You'll be saying next that because there's an opened tin of treacle in Clara's pantry it proves she used some to break the window."

"As a matter of fact, old boy, there isn't any treacle in her pantry—I looked. But she could easily have got rid of it."

"In fact, she's guilty either way . . .! I'm sorry—I think the whole idea's quite preposterous. . . . Apart from anything else, I doubt if Barr would have had time to dispose of a body."

"He'd have been free from half-past six, when Landon arrived, until about a quarter past eight, when he was called to Palmers Road. That's getting on for two hours. Anyone could dispose of a body in two hours, if they knew exactly what they were going to do."

"Has anyone checked on what Barr was supposed to be doing during those two hours?"

"Not yet, but believe me it's high on my list."

"He was probably sitting at home watching TV and wishing he was with Clara. . . . It's no good, I just can't buy it. I simply don't see Clara Waugh as a parricide."

"That's because you don't know her, old boy," Lawson said earnestly. "I do—I told you, I've studied her. I've checked with her neighbours and I've checked with her friends. And if you want my frank opinion, she's not much better than a high-class tart. She started off on the wrong foot with her marriage—her husband divorced her for adultery after seven months and she didn't defend the suit. Some playboy was the co-respondent. And that house in Palmers Road hasn't been exactly a convent, believe me—there's been more than one dark figure creeping out at night by the back way. *And* some pretty wild parties there. At the very best, Clara's a sexy, hard-drinking, good-time girl. That's the consensus of opinion on her, anyway. I'm not surprised her father didn't approve of the way she was carrying on. Do you know she hasn't had a solid job in years? That actress stuff's all baloney. She's had a bit of training, of course—you can tell that from the wonderful act she's been putting on. All those phony dinner preparations, and the sorrow-for-dear-father since! But she's never had any really worthwhile jobs on the stage—just bit parts and the chorus in musicals—that kind of stuff. If our Clara's anything, she's a photographer's model. Here—look at these . . .!" Lawson whisked a couple of postcards out of his pocket and passed them to me with a leer.

"More trophies?" I said.

"That's right."

I looked at them. They were posed photographs of Clara Waugh, as nearly nude as made no odds. There was nothing at all suggestive or indecent about them. I thought they were rather nice.

"Shapely arms she's got!" Lawson said.

"She's got a lovely figure."

"Yes, she's quite a dish. . . . You see what I mean, old boy, don't you?"

"As a matter of fact, I don't. Lots of girls do this sort of thing."

"Ah, but in Clara's case one thing has led to another. . . ." He took the postcards back and put them carefully away in his pocket. "Then we come to Ronald Barr. I've been looking into him pretty closely, too. His background's shrouded in mystery. He's old school tie, to hear him talk, but I don't know where he went to. He's supposed to be some sort of commission agent, and he appears to do quite nicely—pleasant flat, runs a car, dresses well—but if you ask me he's really living by his wits and would find ten thousand pounds most useful as a dowry. He certainly isn't employed regularly by anyone. . . . I can tell you he's not the sort of man I'd want my daughter to marry."

I grinned. "For the sake of the human race, let's hope you never have a daughter."

"I resent that, old boy."

"I never met anyone before with a triple standard of morality, but you've certainly got it—one for women, one for men, and one for Lawson!"

"Okay, you have your little joke. . . . I've got my theory."

"All you've got," I said, "is a lot of unsubstantiated gossip and a hell of an imagination. . . . I think your theory stinks!"

At that moment the News Room door burst open with a crash and someone shouted my name. I hurried in. Blair had a piece of copy in his hand. He looked as though he was about to burst open, too. "Read this, Curtis!" He thrust the copy at me. "My word, this is going to be a great story. . . .! What do you think of it—m'm?—m'm?" He was practically capering.

The copy was an agency "flash," catchlined MISSING SCIENTIST. It said: "A letter was delivered to the Ministry of Supply this morning from the kidnappers of Arthur Landon. The letter said the abduction was a commercial venture and the price of Landon's life would be thirty thousand pounds. The letter was posted in Sheffield between 12.30 p.m. and 2.30 p.m. yesterday."

"Better get along to the Ministry right away, Curtis," Blair said.

I nodded, and went back into the Reporters' Room and grabbed my coat and hat. Lawson had resumed his typing. I stepped up behind him and put the message across his typewriter. "All we need to know now," I said, "is how Barr and Clara posted a letter in Sheffield when they were at a Ministry conference in London!"

There was a moment of silence while Lawson read the message. Then he sighed, and pulled the memorandum out of his machine, and slowly tore it up.

"Okay, old boy, you win!" he said. "Too bad—I thought I was really on to something."

Chapter Four

The Ministry was still comparatively quiet when I got there, but more reporters were rolling up every minute and it wasn't long before the waiting-room was jam-packed. There was no lack of excitement this time, and as the crowd swelled the hubbub grew terrific. Robson came out once and said we'd have to be patient—it seemed that Scotland Yard's laboratory experts were still working on the letter and it might be some time before the tests were finished. Actually it was about an hour. Then we were invited in and the letter was shown to us.

It consisted of a sheet of thin, unwatermarked, quarto-size typing paper, with a message made up of capital letters that had been cut from the smaller headlines of newspapers, and stuck on. It wasn't a very original method of criminal communication, but it was none the less effective for that. According to Bailey, it gave nothing whatever away. The typing paper, he said, could have been bought anywhere and at any time, and was untraceable. There were no fingerprints, which meant that whoever had prepared the message had worn gloves—probably thin surgical gloves, so that the tiny capitals could be easily handled. The gum was the sort you could buy in bottles at any stationer's. The letters were mainly in 24 point, but some in 36. They were in many different founts of type. Some of the type had been identified as the sort in use by particular newspapers, but the knowledge didn't help at all. Cutting the letters out and then sticking them together to form the message would have been a fairly laborious business—the police estimated that it could have taken up to an hour. The envelope was a cheap buff one, of foolscap size—the sort used by the million in business offices. The address on the envelope was simply MINISTRY OF SUPPLY, LONDON, and consisted of the four words cut out whole from newspapers and stuck on. The letter had been posted in a Sheffield pillar-box some time after the 12.30 p.m. collection and before the 2.30 p.m. collection the previous day. It had been delivered by the first post that morning.

The full text of the message ran:

WE HAVE KIDNAPPED ARTHUR LANDON AND ARE HOLDING HIM IN A PLACE WHERE YOU HAVE NO CHANCE OF FINDING HIM. THIS ABDUCTION IS A PURELY COMMERCIAL VENTURE AND WE SHALL RELEASE HIM AT ONCE IF WE ARE PAID THIRTY THOUSAND POUNDS. OTHERWISE WE SHALL KILL HIM. WE SHALL WATCH THE PRESS FOR YOUR REACTIONS.

It was a fascinating document, and at once it set everyone speculating. The first question, obviously, was whether it was genuine. There was no certainty of that—it could easily have been concocted by some practical joker. It didn't *sound* like the kind of letter one usually associated with kidnappers. The *Gazette* man actually suggested that not only the letter but the whole kidnapping might be phony—that it could have been undertaken in a spirit of youthful adventure, like the seizing of the Coronation Stone, but with less point. No one else thought that very likely, but it couldn't be entirely ruled out.

If the whole thing was genuine, then the contents of the letter told us quite a bit more about the kidnappers. In the first place, there were at least two of them. That wasn't surprising, if the purpose of the operation was to hold Landon to ransom and not just to kill him. Murder could be a one-man job; organising a kidnapping and then looking after the prisoner would certainly require at least two. Then, again, they seemed to be a special sort of kidnappers. The tone of the letter was highly literate. The phrasing of the letter was confident and cool—indeed, if its threats were to be taken seriously, chilling. On the face of it, the writers were sophisticated and formidable men who knew exactly what they were about.

There was a further point. It was now clearer than ever that we were dealing with people who had either been very closely associated with Landon or had been primed by someone closely associated with him. They'd not only known about his forthcoming visit to his daughter, and all the circumstances of the visit—they'd also known enough about the nature of his work to feel hopeful that the terrific ransom price of £30,000 wouldn't be too high for someone to pay. They might well have been too hopeful—the general view was that their "commercial venture" was a pretty unpromising one—but at least they must have had something firm to go on. Unfortunately, knowing there'd been a close association didn't help much when it came to picking them out. Further inquiries by the police at Crede, it seemed, had greatly widened the circle of those who'd had all the necessary information. Landon, pleased about his daughter's engagement, had talked freely to his friends about his various visits. Several of the conversations had been in public places and could have been overheard. Any one of several dozen men might have known all that was necessary about the vital visit—and these men were precisely the ones who were closely associated with Landon in his special work and would know the value of it. Any of them could, in theory, have tipped off a couple of kidnappers, with the idea of sharing the loot. It didn't seem probable that they had—but Landon was undoubtedly missing!

The one solid piece of information we had was that the ransom letter had been posted in Sheffield—but that didn't help much, either. Checks were being made at the Crede Establishment, we were told, about the recent movements of personnel, but it was clearly no more than a routine measure. No one really expected that one of Landon's colleagues would turn out to have been in Sheffield the previous day. Even the fact that one, at least, of the kidnappers had been there didn't mean that the Sheffield area was the place to look for Landon. It would have been an obvious precaution to post the letter well away from the hideout. In any case, there could be no effective "looking" without more clues. For the moment, the kidnappers were completely in control of the situation.

We hadn't seen Clara Waugh at the Ministry this time—apparently she'd been called there earlier in the day and been shown the letter and had then left. The time seemed to have come to interview her again, and when I rang the office I expected to be sent straight along to Palmers Road. Instead I was called back, only to find there'd been some mix-up about who was to see her, and that I was to go after all. I got to her house about two-thirty and found her standing on the pavement with Ronald Barr, who was just leaving. Barr said, "Good God, how many more of you?" when he realised I was a reporter. Evidently there'd been quite an invasion. He called to Clara, "See you to-night, darling—keep your chin up!" and waved, and drove away. I introduced myself to Clara and she asked me in. She didn't seem to mind one more reporter—in fact I had the impression she was quite glad of any company. She looked strained and tired, but she had herself well in hand. There were some bottles and used glasses on a tray in the sitting-room, and I guessed she'd been fortifying herself. Considering the contents of that letter, I didn't blame her.

The interview went very smoothly, because she'd already been over all the ground with the others. I asked her if she felt the ransom letter was genuine and she said she hadn't much doubt that it was. I asked her what she thought about it.

"Well," she said, "in a way it's a tremendous relief, because at least it means that Father's still alive, and I wasn't at all sure about that. . . . But I don't know what's going to happen—it's such a fantastic lot of money they're asking for."

I agreed that it was. "Has your father got any wealthy friends?" I asked. "People who might club together, perhaps . . .?"

She shook her head in a weary gesture. "I don't think he knew anyone wealthy at all. Most of his friends are scientists, and they don't get very much money. Father certainly didn't—not the kind

41

of money these people are interested in. He had enough for his needs, but that was all."

"What about you? No wealthy friends?"

She gave a wry smile. "I dare say I could borrow twenty pounds if I was very hard pushed."

"Do you think the Government should pay the ransom—assuming the letter turns out to be genuine?"

"Well, of course I do—it's the only hope. *And* it's only fair. Father's worked terrifically hard for them, and it's only because of the work he was doing that he's in this awful position now."

"Do you think they *will* pay?"

"I don't know. I *hope* they will. . . . But I'm terribly afraid."

I gave a sympathetic nod. If I'd been her, I'd have been afraid, too! I asked her one or two more questions and then got up to leave. I said I hoped things would turn out all right for her. There wasn't much else I could say. She said, "Thank you!—let's hope so." She walked with me to my car. She had a most graceful walk—her figure was a dream. When I looked at her I couldn't help remembering that damned postcard of Lawson's!

That afternoon a tremendous political rumpus broke out over Landon. It was the *Evening Post* that started it. I never learned for certain where it got its information from, but its editor, a brilliant man named Max Waller, was known to be a close personal friend of Sir Maurice Proude, Landon's administrative chief, and maybe Proude, desperately concerned about Landon's safety, committed a calculated indiscretion. Anyway, that afternoon the *Post* published a piece by its Political Correspondent and a strong supporting editorial, virtually accusing the Government of having wilfully misled the country about Landon's importance in the security set-up. According to the *Post's* information, Landon had been the lynch-pin in an ambitious project for the defence of the country against high-speed rocket attack. Without Landon, the *Post* said, the solution of this most vital of all defence problems would be set back perhaps by years. It was precisely because of his unique gifts, which in his specialised field amounted to genius, that he had been given exceptional protection—and for the same reason, that his kidnapping had seemed worth while. The Minister of Supply, the *Post* declared, had underrated the gravity of the situation, not for reasons of security but to cover up official blundering.

It was a terrific attack, and of course there was a terrific row. In the House that afternoon the Opposition raked the Supply Minister fore and aft, and he took a lot of punishment. At first he was inclined to bluster, hinting that the *Post* might well have exposed itself to proceedings under the Official Secrets Act, but that didn't get him anywhere. He naturally wouldn't confirm the *Post's* story, but he didn't deny it, either, and by the time he sat down there wasn't an M.P. who didn't believe it to be true. The Government's supporters were by now as worried as the Opposition, and several of them wanted to know the Government's view of the ransom letter that had arrived that day, and what it proposed to do about it. In the end, the Prime Minister intervened to make a statement. He reminded the House that the genuineness of the letter had not yet been established. Even if it were, he said, the Government had no doubt of its duty. Arthur Landon was a valued public servant, a man of exceptional brilliance in his field, and it was true that the importance of his work to the country could hardly be overestimated. But no Government could pay ransom money to criminals. If it did, that would be an invitation to others to follow their example, and it would be the beginning of the end of law and order. What the Government could say was that no stone would be left unturned to trace the kidnappers and release Landon. If anything happened to him, no efforts would be spared to apprehend and punish the guilty men.... It was a pompous and cliché-ridden statement, yet it was hard to find fault with the sentiments. At least, that was my feeling when I read it.

Next morning, though, the Press was by no means unanimous on the point. The more sober papers backed the Government, but two of the popular dailies with the largest circulations took the view that it would be disastrous folly to risk losing a man like Landon if thirty thousand pounds could secure his freedom, and that the public interest required a much more realistic attitude.

Would a Government refuse to pay kidnappers in time of war, one of them asked, if the safety of some vitally important person were at stake?—and was not the present state of the world almost as dangerous as though we were at war? In any case, if the Government found it impossible to meet the demand on grounds of principle, were there no unofficial bodies who would take responsibility for paying the ransom money?

That was one aspect of the discussion—what might be called the moral side. But alongside it, every paper was vigorously debating the *feasibility* of securing Landon's release by paying the ransom. Cases were cited where large ransoms had been paid to kidnappers by friends and relatives without any subsequent release of the person kidnapped. Often the victim had later been discovered dead. It had to be borne in mind that by now Landon would know and be able to describe his captors, and that in those circumstances it was gravely open to doubt whether they would ever dare to release him. The morning's debate must have made melancholy reading for Clara.

The argument raged all day, involving pretty well everyone. The pubs were noisier with altercation than I'd known them for a long time. There were people for action, and people against it, but by now there seemed to be virtual agreement on two points—that the results of losing Landon could scarcely be more serious for the country; and that if the ransom *wasn't* paid he probably hadn't got a hope. It was only too obvious that the police were completely in the dark and had nothing whatever to go on. The slightest slip-up by the kidnappers might give them their opportunity but until then they were powerless—and there was no good reason to expect any slip-up. Wherever the kidnappers had hidden Landon, it must be somewhere pretty safe, because by now his face was as well known to the public as though he'd been a TV announcer and the whole country had been urged to keep watch for any out-of-the-ordinary incident that might give a clue to his whereabouts. And there just hadn't been any. The dangerous time for the kidnappers had been the night of his abduction. Having survived that, having got Landon under cover, all they had to do was sit tight and wait.

I was sent out of town that night on an entirely different story, so I didn't hear the big news till I got back next day. It was sensational. Two more letters had arrived at the Ministry by the first post that morning, and one of them was from Landon himself. Clara had been called in to identify the handwriting, which she'd had no difficulty in doing. The letter had been written with a ball-point pen, on the same sort of typing paper as the first message from the kidnappers. It had said:

"I am being well-treated and I am in good health, I have read what the newspapers have written—that my abductors will kill me in the end because I could describe them. I wish to say that both of them have worn face-coverings in my presence on all occasions and that up to now I could not describe them. If it is decided to pay the ransom money, therefore, I see no reason why they should kill me. Otherwise, they say they will, and I'm afraid they may mean it. I have written this of my own volition, in an effort to help myself. I am not allowed to say anything more. Arthur Landon."

The second letter had been made up of newspaper capitals, as before, and had said tersely:

LANDON WILL BE KILLED AT MIDNIGHT NEXT TUESDAY IF THE THIRTY THOUSAND POUNDS HAS NOT BEEN PAID BY THEN. WE SHALL CONTINUE TO WATCH THE PRESS FOR SIGNS OF A SENSIBLE RESPONSE.

The two letters had been sent separately, each in the same sort of foolscap envelope as before. The envelope containing Landon's letter had been addressed in his own handwriting, the other in gummed capitals. Both had been posted in a box at Staines, Middlesex, some time between the last collection the previous evening, which had been at 7.30, and the first that day, which had been at 8 a.m.

There was one thing at least that we didn't have to wonder about any more. We knew now that the kidnapping was genuine and the danger deadly and imminent. But there was plenty of fresh ground for speculation. Could Landon's letter be taken at its face value, or had he been forced to write what he had? Had he really not seen the face of his captors? On the whole, the view was that he hadn't. The handwriting was firm. It didn't look like the sort of letter a man was being forced to write under some immediate threat. You could dictate a calm-sounding, well-composed letter, but you couldn't force a man's hand to be steady as he wrote it down. The more you threatened, the less steady it would be. So this, presumably, was the genuine Landon, telling the truth. And if the kidnappers *had* taken the trouble to keep their faces covered all the time, that seemed a hopeful sign, for it suggested that they'd always intended to release Landon in return for payment, and had planned for it.

Why Staines? Staines was near London, on the way to the West. Sheffield had been in the North. The likeliest answer, once again, seemed to be that neither place had any special significance. The unknown kidnappers were free to travel all over the country at will, provided Landon's prison was secure, so they could post their messages anywhere. Variety would help to confuse the police, and give nothing away. There was certainly no slip-up yet.

It was in the late afternoon that the office grapevine began to whisper of dramatic new events. Something, one gathered, was afoot. Sensitive antennae recorded strange goings-on. The Editor was known to have had a specially important lunch and no one could say with whom. Several of the senior executives had been called in to see him at unusual times. The chairman and one of the directors had been seen on their way up to the Board Room, though there was not normally a Board Meeting on Thursdays. The afternoon news conference was presided over by the Assistant Editor, which was rare on a weekday. By five o'clock, the privileged few who knew were discussing the matter conspiratorially in corridors. By six, the news was out. The *Record* was going to offer to pay the ransom money!

It was a daring publicity idea—full of hazards, but likely to be most productive of goodwill if it came off. By now majority opinion in the country was undoubtedly in favour of some sort of action, and I thought we'd been pretty smart to get in before the other papers. I was supposed to be off duty at seven but I couldn't tear myself away from the office and when the early edition of the paper came up soon after ten I grabbed a copy eagerly. The announcement was made in bold type on the front page. The *Record* it said, would make one payment of £30,000 to the kidnappers in return for their undertaking to release Landon. It would be paid in accordance with any reasonable instructions from the kidnappers, and the Editor was ready to receive those instructions in any way the kidnappers cared to convey them.

On an inside page, there was an article by the Editor himself, explaining the paper's action to our two million readers. The decision had been taken, he wrote, in the public interest, because we believed the country could not afford to sacrifice Landon. The offer was being made with a full sense of responsibility, and after the most careful consideration of all the issues involved. The Board realised that their decision would arouse controversy and that some people would be against it. They did not pretend that there was not another side to the question. It was repugnant to have to bargain with criminals, but the Board believed that this was an exceptional occasion. The *Record* yielded place to no one in condemning the outrageous crime that had been committed, and once Landon was released it would do all in its power to help bring the criminals to justice. The Board were aware that there was no certainty that Landon would in fact be released, but they believed that the chance must be taken and were prepared to pay for their belief. . . . It was a good article, frank and persuasive. Reading it, I could almost believe myself that our sole interest in the matter was to get Landon freed!

There was tremendous excitement about it in Fleet Street next day. All the other papers had reported our offer, since it was unquestionably news—but in much smaller type. Privately, comment was cynical, both about our motives and our prospects. Most of the people I talked to thought we'd merely lose £30,000. Some thought we should have offered the money only in direct exchange for Landon—a condition which I gathered we'd refrained from making because it would almost certainly be rejected by the kidnappers as too hazardous for them. There was some interesting speculation about how the kidnappers would get in touch with us, if they decided to do so. There was no criticism of the offer in the other papers, on the principle that dog doesn't eat dog. Also, it was assumed that we hadn't made the decision without taking top-level advice, and that tacitly the Cabinet was probably behind us. There was even a school of thought that believed the whole thing had been concerted between the *Record* and the police and that we were actually helping to lay a trap for the kidnappers.

Apart from the feverish discussion, the day passed quietly, with no further news. The next day, Saturday, I was off duty, and I drove down into Surrey to lunch with my people. I got back to Chancery Lane about six. There was nothing fresh about the case in the evening papers. I thought I'd call up Mollie and see what she was doing and I was just going to pick up the telephone when it rang. It was the office. Parker was on the Desk. He said, "Hugh!—could you come in and see the Editor right away?"

I said, "The *Editor*!" This was Saturday evening. The Editor never went near the office on a Saturday unless a war was about to break out. I said, "What's happened?"—though I think I knew before he told me.

"We've had a letter," Parker said.

Chapter Five

It took me less than five minutes to reach the office. As always, on a Saturday evening, the place was as silent as a morgue. Except for Sergeant Stubbins, the commissionaire on duty at the front box, Parker was the only man in the building. I joined him in the News Room. The Editor, he told me, was on his way round—he'd been waiting at his flat until he'd heard that the office had been able to contact me.

I said, "When did the letter come?"

"By the afternoon post. I'm not *sure* it's from the kidnappers—the address was in ordinary written capitals, not the usual stuck-on stuff—but I think it must be. Blair went off in a taxi with it to the Editor right away—and there's obviously something up."

We discussed it for a moment or two. Then there was a brisk step in the corridor and the Editor put his head in. "Ah, you're here, Curtis!" he said. "Come along, will you?" I followed him to his room at the end of the passage. He switched on the lights and an electric wall fire, and motioned me to a chair.

The Editor's name was Grant—John Grant. He was a very tall, lanky man, with a lean, aquiline face and a lantern jaw. His age was about forty-five. He wasn't actually a professional newspaperman at all—not by training. He'd come to the *Record* via economic journalism, of all things—helped, perhaps, by the fact that he'd been a Colonel in Military Intelligence during the war, and knew the chairman well, and had a lot of high-up friends. But if he was only an amateur he was an enthusiastic and gifted one, and he gave the impression of enjoying every minute in his editorial chair. He was original in his views, unorthodox in his ways, and slightly sardonic in his manner. He'd come in for the usual professional criticism from time to time because he hadn't started as the office-boy and worked his way up, but of course it didn't worry him. By any reckoning he was quite a personality. I'd had more to do with him than a reporter usually has with an editor, as a result of a couple of sensational stories I'd covered in Sussex and Cornwall, and I'd always got on with him excellently.

"Well," he said, with a faint grin, "I expect you've a pretty good idea what this is all about?"

"I gather we've had a letter," I said.

"We have, indeed. . . . Take a look at it." He tossed a sheet of paper across the desk, with an envelope attached to it. The letter was the usual gummed-up concoction on typing paper, only this time there was much more of it. Somebody had been having a real session. It said:

WE ACCEPT YOUR OFFER. HERE ARE YOUR INSTRUCTIONS. PAYMENT IS TO BE MADE IN USED FIVE-POUND NOTES. THEY ARE TO BE BROUGHT TO THE RENDEZVOUS BY A RELIABLE REPORTER OF THE DAILY RECORD. HE IS TO BE ACCOMPANIED BY LANDON'S DAUGHTER, CLARA WAUGH. SINCE SHE IS THE ONLY PERSON WHO CAN BE TRUSTED TO PUT HER FATHER'S SAFETY ABOVE EVERYTHING ELSE, WE REGARD HER PRESENCE AS THE ONLY ADEQUATE GUARANTEE THAT NO TRICKS WILL BE ATTEMPTED, AND IT IS A CONDITION OF THE SETTLEMENT. NO ONE ELSE IS TO COME. AT THE FIRST SIGN OF ANY DOUBLE-DEALING, LANDON WILL BE KILLED AND WE SHALL DISAPPEAR FOR GOOD. THE RENDEZVOUS IS A BROKEN NOTICE BOARD AT THE FOOT OF MAM TOR PRECIPICE NEAR CASTLETON IN DERBYSHIRE. IT MUST NOT BE DISCLOSED TO ANYONE EXCEPT YOUR REPORTER AND MRS. WAUGH. THE TIME APPOINTED FOR THE MEETING IS 8 P.M. ON

MONDAY NEXT MARCH 21ST. YOUR REPORTER AND MRS. WAUGH MUST ARRIVE EXACTLY ON TIME. THEY ARE TO BRING THE MONEY IN A STRONG SUITCASE WITH A GOOD HANDLE. ON ARRIVAL THEY ARE TO SIGNAL THEIR PRESENCE BY SHINING A TORCH. THEY WILL RECEIVE ALL OTHER NECESSARY INSTRUCTIONS AT THE TIME. LANDON WILL BE RELEASED WITHIN APPROXIMATELY TWENTY-FOUR HOURS OF THE TRANSFER OF THE MONEY. THIS WILL GIVE US TIME TO MAKE SURE THE NOTES ARE NOT MARKED. IF YOU ACCEPT THESE CONDITIONS, LET THE WORD AGREE APPEAR IN THE FIRST PARAGRAPH OF YOUR LEADING ARTICLE ON MONDAY MORNING. OTHERWISE THIS WILL BE OUR LAST COMMUNICATION AND THE LAST ANYONE WILL HEAR OF LANDON. HIS LIFE IS IN YOUR KEEPING.

I looked at the postmark on the envelope. It had been posted overnight at Saffron Walden, a town in Essex about forty miles from London. The kidnappers were evidently continuing to get around. The envelope was addressed to The Editor, Daily Record, Fleet Street, London, in carefully-formed capitals written with a ball-point pen. In the corner, also in large capitals, were the words PERSONAL AND URGENT.

One way and another, the message struck me as a pretty spine-chilling document, as well as a highly melodramatic one. There were a dozen comments and questions in my mind, but only one that couldn't wait till later.

I said, "As you've asked me here, I assume you'd like *me* to take the money up."

"I'd like you to, yes," Grant said. "You've done most of the work on the Landon story up to now—and on past form you should be able to take care of yourself. But this isn't an ordinary assignment, and you're absolutely free to turn it down. I'll want your pledge of silence if you do, that's all." He paused for a moment.

"I don't really think there should be any serious danger, or I wouldn't suggest your going—but it's bound to be a bit nerve-racking. Apart from anything else, you'll be carrying thirty thousand pounds in notes with you, which is enough to scare anyone! Then again, that letter speaks of a 'meeting'—it seems you'll actually be coming face to face with the kidnappers, not just taking the money and leaving it in an appointed place. It'll be quite dark by eight, of course—there's no moon on Monday, I've checked that—and presumably the kidnappers will keep well covered up, but if anything happened so that you *were* in a position to describe them. . . ." He broke off. "Well, they're obviously pretty desperate characters. . . . If you'd like a little time to think it over, I'll understand."

"I don't think I'll need much time," I said, "but there is one thing I'd like to clear up. . . . There's talk in the Street that we're working in with the authorities and simply helping to set a trap. Is that true?"

"It's absolutely untrue. For the time being, we're not interested in catching the kidnappers. Our sole aim is to get Landon back—and we're working entirely on our own."

"Won't the police have to know about this letter?"

"They'll know of its existence, but they won't know its contents. All that part of the thing has been cleared at a high level. We're being given a free hand to get Landon back if we can—and we shall keep strictly to the conditions."

I was silent for a moment. Then I said, "The kidnappers can't know that, of course. I'm astonished they seem so ready to trust us."

"Well, they've insured themselves as far as they can by insisting that Landon's daughter is there too. . . . A very astute move, that!"

"They can't be *certain* she's going to be there, until the actual meeting."

"I wouldn't be too sure, Curtis. One of them may already be keeping a close eye on her."

I rather doubted that—but it was possible.

"Well," I said, "I'm quite ready to take the job on, of course—in fact, I wouldn't miss it for anything.... What about Clara Waugh, though? Have you asked her?"

"Not yet, but I telephoned her and she's coming along here—she should be arriving any minute.... I don't think there's the slightest doubt she'll go with you—I had a letter from her only this morning, thanking us for putting up the money and saying how desperately anxious she was about her father.... Well, now, is there anything else on your mind before she comes?"

There were several things. I said, "I suppose the kidnappers didn't want to use newspaper capitals for the address this time in case the post office people spotted it and passed it straight on to the police?"

"I imagine that's it," Grant agreed.

"I'm rather surprised they didn't just drop it in here by hand."

"They couldn't have known for certain that the police hadn't set a watch on the office."

"That's true, of course...."

"And they certainly couldn't have risked telephoning all that stuff.... I think they probably chose the safest way."

I returned to the letter. "I don't quite get this business of waiting twenty-four hours to make sure the notes aren't marked. Would they be able to tell, if it was done skilfully?"

"I'd have said not ... I thought that was a bit strange myself."

"What's the point, anyway? After all, if we wanted to we could keep a record of the serial numbers."

"Exactly."

"Are we going to?"

"In fact, no. Time's so short, it could only be done by putting a large staff on the job on Monday morning, and there could be a leak. 'The ears of the enemy ...' you know. In any case, they're bound to wait till they think the heat's off before they dispose of the notes, so there's not much point."

"They're taking a big risk for a long-delayed return, aren't they?"

"Well, the whole thing's obviously a tremendous gamble."

I nodded. "There's another rather odd thing here—why all this emphasis on a strong suitcase with a good handle?"

"Six thousand fivers will be quite a load," Grant said.

"Yes, but we hardly need telling that. . . . Still, I suppose they know what they're up to. They certainly give the impression of having everything completely taped."

"Including our leader column!" Grant said, with a grin. "I agree—they seem most efficient. Intelligent and imaginative, too. . . . Not at all the types you'd associate with crude violence."

I was still looking at the letter. "The rendezvous isn't so far away from Sheffield, where the first message was posted. I wonder if there's any significance in that?"

"It's an interesting point," Grant said. "By the way, do you know the place?—Mam Tor?"

"No—I once spent a day at Castleton, but I don't remember Mam Tor. It must be quite easy to find, or they'd have given more detailed directions. . . . What do you suggest I do—drive up on Monday?"

"I should think so, and fairly late. You won't want to be hanging about up there with all that money. In any case we shan't be able to get the notes till the banks open, not without a lot of fuss—and we don't want more of that than we can help."

I said, "Of course, we can't hope to keep this a secret—the fact that a ransom letter has arrived, I mean. It's been guessed at in the office—to-morrow it'll be all over Fleet Street."

"I realise that, but as long as the details aren't known I don't think it matters. I'm taking certain steps. . . ."

At that moment the phone rang. Grant picked up the receiver and I heard Sergeant Stubbins's voice—the commissionaire always had to work the switchboard on Saturday nights. I thought he was probably announcing Clara Waugh's arrival, but he wasn't. Grant said, "*Proude?*—all right, put him through," and waited, frowning. There was a click and another voice spoke. Grant's frown deepened. Suddenly he gestured to me across the desk to listen in on the extension. I picked the phone up quietly. A man's voice, very low-pitched and rather muffled, said, ". . . clearly understood we meant every word we wrote about no tricks. No one is to know anything of the arrangements—not even Clara Waugh's fiancé. I repeat—Landon's life is in your hands. That's all." There was another click, and the line went dead. There'd been no time to try and trace the call, even if we'd wanted to.

Grant hung up, looking a bit shaken. "Well, that brings it home, I must say. . . ." He reached for a cigarette, and lit it, and threw the packet across to me. "It's the first time I've had a kidnapper actually threatening murder in my ear. . . ."

"Did he say he was Sir Maurice Proude?"

"Yes, he's got a nerve, hasn't he? Sense of humour, too, of an impudent kind. . . . What did you make of the voice?"

"It sounded very much like the one Clara Waugh described—the man who made the bogus call to her. Deep, low and muffled. I should think he covered the mouthpiece with something. . . . Could we check if it was a local call?"

Grant gave a nod, and himself called the commissionaire. He got his answer almost at once. The call had originated in the London dialling area. That was all that could be discovered about it.

Suddenly I had another thought—a rather disturbing one. I said, "I wonder how he knew you were at the office—on a Saturday night?"

Grant stared at me. "Apart from my wife," he said slowly, "the only person who knew I was coming here was—Clara Waugh."

"Perhaps he rang you at home first?"

"I'll check. . . ." Grant asked for a line and called his flat. At once I could tell by his tone that someone *had* rung there. After a moment he said, "All right, darling, thanks. No, I shan't be late. 'Bye!" He hung up. "The same man called—said he was the Duty Officer at the Ministry of Supply! My wife suggested he should ring here. . . . Never mind, it was worth trying."

Almost at once the phone went again. This time it *was* Clara, and Stubbins was told to bring her up right away. Grant shook hands with her as she came in, and said he understood that she and I had met, and she said we had and gave me a pale smile. Then Grant found her a comfortable chair and told her we'd had the letter and gave it to her to read.

She read it through carefully and slowly, her face very tense. She looked as though she couldn't quite believe it, which wasn't surprising. At the end, she said in a voice she couldn't keep entirely steady, "Do you really think they'll let him go?"

"I think there's quite a good chance," Grant said. "They must realise they haven't a hope of getting any more money out of anyone after this. They can't *want* to harm your father—it would only make things a lot worse for them if they were ever caught. So I really don't see why they shouldn't set him free."

"Oh, if only they would . . .!"

"The thing is, Mrs. Waugh, are you willing to go with Mr. Curtis here to take the money? That's what I wanted to see you about."

"But of course. I'd do anything—*anything*..... I'm entirely in your hands."

"Not entirely, I'm afraid. Up to a point, you'll be in *their* hands. The last thing I want to do is frighten you, but I think you ought to realise just what you'll be doing. If everything goes smoothly, I don't think there'll be any danger. But you'll be meeting unscrupulous men at night in what sounds a very desolate spot and you'll have thirty thousand pounds with you. It *could* be dangerous."

Clara seemed scarcely to be listening. "Nothing could be worse than waiting and not knowing. . . . I'll take any risk if it'll help."

"Good!" Grant said. "I thought you would. . . . Now there's one other point. A few minutes before you came in, one of the kidnappers telephoned. . . ."

Clara stared at him. "Rang up here!"

"Yes. . . . It was a bit of a shock for us, too, wasn't it, Curtis? We think it was the same man who gave you the bogus message about the hospital. Anyway, he rang to underline the warning he gives in that letter—that no one must be told where you're going on Monday."

Clara nodded. "I realise that. I certainly shan't tell anyone."

"He said not even your fiancé. He made a particular point of that."

"Oh . . . I see!" She looked troubled. "I suppose I probably *would* have told him. . . ."

"It would be better not to, Mrs. Waugh."

"But he wouldn't breathe a word. . . ."

"I'm quite sure he wouldn't—I'm sure he'd be discretion itself. But your father's life is at stake, and it's better not to take the slightest risk. You'll forgive me, won't you . . .?"

"Of course," she said. "I understand. But it won't be easy not to tell him. We've been together practically the whole time since Father's disappearance—I've relied on him absolutely. I'm afraid he'll be terribly hurt when he finds out. . . ."

"I don't think so," Grant said gently. "I think he'll understand, too."

"But he's bound to want to know where I'm going—I'll have to tell him *something*. . . ."

"I'm sure you'll be able to think of a convincing story. It'll be in a good cause."

"Well, I'll try," she said. "I don't like it much—but I'll do my best."

"Good! Then that's really all, Mrs. Waugh. The vital thing, remember, is not to talk about it to *anyone*—not a word. Mr. Curtis will be getting in touch with you, probably on Monday morning, to tell you what the arrangements are. . . ." Grant smiled. "All right?"

"Of course—and thank you so much again, Mr. Grant, for everything you're doing. I'm deeply grateful."

"Let's hope we pull it off," Grant said.

Chapter Six

We'd been right not to count on keeping secret the significance of the letter we'd received. By noon next day, every newspaper in Fleet Street was taking it for granted we'd had a reply from the kidnappers. The assumptions didn't stop there, either. Everyone at the *Record* was speculating about the next step, and the chain of logic was simple. The kidnappers must have sent their instructions about the handing over of the money. Someone would have to take it to them on behalf of the *Record*. I'd been on the story—and I'd been called into the office on a Saturday to see the Editor. Conclusion—I was going to be the courier. The gossip soon spread through the Street—but no one really knew for certain, and in any case it didn't matter. All the other papers had suddenly developed a discreet inactivity over the story—so much so that I felt sure Grant had been phoning around and arranging a truce with their editors on grounds of public interest. That meant I wasn't going to be troubled at all by rival sleuths. At the *Record* itself I came in for a good deal of light banter, but I didn't admit anything. I said brazenly that my call to the Editor on Saturday had been about quite a different aspect of the Landon case, and that if any reporter was sent with the money it would probably be Hunt, since he was the chief reporter and a man of great experience—or else Lawson, because he was the crime reporter and was used to associating with crooks! That started a minor flap. They must have known I was kidding, but I'd managed to sow a tiny seed of doubt, all the same. Hunt said he'd been suffering from rheumatism in his right leg all week, and by the end of the day he was noticeably limping. Lawson was still more worried, and not even Parker's remark that only a lunatic would trust Lawson with thirty thousand pounds set his mind completely at rest. One way and another, it was quite an amusing morning.

The afternoon passed quietly. There were no preparations that I needed to make until the next day, and to all outward appearances I did a normal spell of duty. Blair played up by giving me a routine job or two. He must have been told I'd been earmarked to take the money, but no one would have guessed it from his manner.

Then, just after six, I was called to the phone. It was Clara on the line. She said, "Oh, Mr. Curtis, I'm so glad you're there.... I tried to get Mr. Grant, but they couldn't find him...." She sounded on the verge of tears. "Is it all right to talk?"

I thought of the switchboard girls. "No," I said, "I don't think it is ... Are you at home?"

"Yes."

"Then you'd better hang up, and I'll call you back straight away."

She said, "All right," and put the receiver down. I went out into the corridor, where there was a public call-box, and dialled her number, and she answered at once.

"Okay," I said, "now we can talk freely. What's the trouble?"

"I'm afraid Ronald's found out—about the meeting. He's in a furious temper about it—he's on his way to see Mr. Grant now. He says it's too dangerous. I thought I'd better warn you...."

"I don't get it," I said. "You mean you told him?"

"No, of course not ... It all happened because that man phoned *me* this afternoon—the kidnapper. He started to warn *me* about not telling anyone ... Ronald was here with me. I told the man he'd got the wrong number and rang off but he called again and it was all terribly awkward and Ronald got suspicious. I'd already said I thought it might be a good idea if I went to stay with a girl friend for a day or two and he'd seemed hurt and puzzled—and this just finished it. He began to ask me a lot of questions and—well, in the end he just guessed I was involved with the *Record* over the money, and we had a frightful row, and he said he was going to have it out with Mr. Grant right away ... I'm terribly sorry—I did my best."

"How *much* does he know?"

"Oh, no details at all. I didn't tell him a thing—I wouldn't even admit that I was going. That was what made him so angry."

"Well, it doesn't sound as though there's much harm done," I said. "As long as you're still game to come with me."

"But of course. Wild horses wouldn't stop me."

"Then we'll sort things out here, and I'll ring you later."

I hung up, and went straight along to tell Grant. He was back in his room from wherever he'd been and was sitting with his long legs up on the desk, reading a galley proof. I'd rushed in without much ceremony and he looked a bit surprised. "Something wrong, Curtis?"

I told him about the kidnapper's call, and what had happened.

His legs came down with a crash. "*Damn!*" he said. "The idiots! Why on earth couldn't they leave well alone . . .?"

"They must be more nervous than we thought."

"They certainly must . . .!"

"The thing is," I said, "what are we going to do about Barr? I gather he may be here any minute."

"There's only one thing we can do, now—admit that Clara's going with you, and try to make him see reason. Otherwise he may give endless trouble. Don't you agree?"

"Well, yes, I do."

"Right. . . ." Grant got up and began to pace about the room. "You know, I had a feeling something like this might happen. Clara didn't look as though deceit was going to come easy to her."

"She's supposed to be an actress," I said. "I'm disappointed in her."

"Ah, well, it can't be so easy putting on an act when you're involved yourself. . . ."

At that moment the phone rang in the ante-room. Miss Wharton, Grant's secretary, popped her head in. "There's a Mr. Barr asking if he can see you, Mr. Grant."

Grant nodded. "Have him brought up right away. . . . You'd better sit in on this interview, Curtis."

In a couple of minutes Barr was shown in. He ignored Grant's hand. He didn't appear to recognise me at all. Grant introduced me, and he gave a curt nod. He looked pretty formidable, with his cold blue eyes and his craggy chin. He was obviously in a foul temper. "I've come to see you," he began, "because——"

Grant interrupted him. "I know, Mr. Barr. Mrs. Waugh has been on the phone to us. It'll probably simplify things if I tell you right away that Mrs. Waugh *has* undertaken to be present when the money is handed over to Landon's kidnappers. That's what she's going to do to-morrow. She's agreed to accompany Mr. Curtis to the rendezvous."

"I thought that was it . . .! Well, I can tell you here and now that it's out of the question."

Grant said quietly, "Wouldn't it be better if we discussed this like reasonable people . . .? Why not have a chair?"

"No thank you."

"As you please. . . . The position is this, Mr. Barr. The kidnappers have made Mrs. Waugh's presence a condition of releasing Landon. From their point of view it's an understandable safeguard, and we have to accept it. If she doesn't go, there'll be no deal. . . . I assume you want her father to be freed?"

"A good deal more than you do, I dare say."

"What exactly do you mean by that?"

"Just that I don't believe Landon's your first consideration—or anyone else's, except Clara's. For you, this is just a publicity stunt, and for the police, it's a way of trying to catch the kidnappers. I wasn't born yesterday! You don't suppose anyone really believes you're going to hand over thirty thousand pounds, just like that, and trust to luck that Landon will be freed afterwards? It's a trap, of course, and if the kidnappers find out before they're caught it could be a damned dangerous one for all concerned. I'm just not standing for it."

Grant sighed. "I give you my personal assurance, Mr. Barr, my word of honour, that what you've just said is not true. We are not co-operating with the police, and there's no trap. As far as we're concerned, the whole thing is strictly on the level."

Barr stared at him. "You can't really mean that?"

"It's the truth. Good heavens, man, do you suppose Mrs. Waugh would have agreed to come in with us if she'd thought we were merely interested in catching the kidnappers? It's her father she's thinking about."

"Of course, but she could be deceived. She doesn't know what's going on behind the scenes."

"She'll know before the meeting takes place. A trap means people around, a lot of people. The fact couldn't possibly be hidden from her. And as the kidnappers have sworn to kill her father at the first sign of any tricks, she obviously wouldn't carry on. I repeat, there is going to be no trap, either now or later. We're not even going to try and trace the money. We're going to play fair, and hope the kidnappers will too."

Barr said, "Oh!" and dropped into a chair. Grant followed up his advantage. "Our only interest is to get Landon set free," he said, "and the simple fact is that if Mrs. Waugh doesn't help us we haven't a chance."

"I doubt if you've a chance anyway," Barr said.

"That remains to be seen. We think we have."

"If you have, it's so slim that you're not justified in risking Clara's safety over it. Even if this thing *is* on the level, there's bound to be danger."

"There shouldn't be any serious danger."

"You can't possibly know that. The men you're dealing with sound like the kind that don't draw the line anywhere. I'd say they're quite capable of taking your money, and then shooting Clara and Curtis and Landon as well. From their point of view, what could be better than a nice tidy silence behind them?"

"I understand your feelings . . ." Grant said.

"So you should," Barr said with heat. "Damn it, I'm in love with Clara—we're going to be married directly this business is over. She means everything to me. Would you let your wife go off with thirty thousand pounds for a quiet meeting with a couple of desperadoes?"

"I say again that you're exaggerating the danger. . . ." Grant's manner had become a little stiff. "In any case, I feel bound to point out that Mrs. Waugh isn't a child—nor yet even your wife. She's an adult, independent woman who's more concerned at this moment about getting her father back alive than about anything else on earth. She's upset about your attitude, but our information is that her own hasn't changed, and I frankly doubt if anything would persuade her to abandon this undertaking now. All you're doing, if you'll forgive my saying so, is to make things more difficult for her. I don't think you'll change her decision. And if you can't change hers, you certainly won't change ours."

It was a forceful speech, and Barr looked a bit abashed. Grant continued:

"As I see it, Mr. Barr, your fiancée's future happiness depends to a very large extent on the success of this enterprise. If she abandoned it out of fear, and these men killed her father, I doubt if she'd ever forgive herself—or you. Surely you can see that? It's a tough situation—worse for you than for her, I agree—but it's a situation where you ought to look ahead and weigh all the risks, not just the immediate ones."

Barr was silent for a while. Presently he said, in a more conciliatory tone, "Where is this meeting going to take place?"

"That I can't tell you. I can't tell you anything about it at all. I've been specifically warned not to. The details are known, literally, only to Mr. Curtis—who's the acceptable representative of the paper—to Mrs. Waugh, and to myself. And that, I'm afraid, is how it must remain."

"You surely don't suppose *I'd* talk?"

"I shouldn't think so for a moment—but a secret is a secret."

"All right," Barr said, "keep your secret. . . . But is there any reason why I shouldn't be taken along at the time? I'd feel very different about the thing if I was there too."

"It's impossible, Mr. Barr. The conditions are that Mrs. Waugh should go with a *Record* reporter, and that there should be no one else there at all."

"But would the kidnappers know? Surely this meeting isn't to take place in daylight?"

"I can't tell you when the meeting's to take place."

"Well, it must be after dark unless they're crazy. And if it's after dark they wouldn't even see me. I'd keep well back, right out of the way, as long as I wasn't needed."

Grant shook his head. "It's far, far too risky. We've no idea what the circumstances will be at the meeting. We don't know where, or how, these men will be watching. We don't know when the watching may start. Our only safe course, if we want results, is to follow our instructions to the letter—and that's what we're going to do."

I said, "May I say something?"

"Sure—go ahead."

I turned to Barr. "I just wanted to tell you that I'll look after Mrs. Waugh as though she were my own girl. I can't promise absolute safety for either of us—but you can rely on me to do everything I can."

Barr looked me up and down, and what he saw must have been reasonably reassuring. The hard glint went out of his eyes, and he gave a little nod.

"You certainly look tough enough," he said. He swung round to Grant. "Well, I don't seem to have much choice, do I? I still don't like the idea—I just hate the thought of Clara going off without me. I hate the whole thing—and I'll be very surprised if it works. But you're probably right that I couldn't dissuade her now. . . . And I certainly wouldn't want her to think I was responsible if anything happened to her father. So—okay!"

"Good man!" Grant said. "I don't believe you'll regret it. . . . Will you tell Mrs. Waugh yourself, or shall we?"

"I'll tell her." Barr got up, and held out his hand to me. "The best of luck, then, Curtis. . . . I *do* rely on you. Clara's had a pretty tough time already—I don't think she can stand much more. . . . Good-bye, sir." He shook hands with Grant, and left.

There was a little silence after he'd gone. Then Grant said, "Obstinate chap . . .! Still, I must say I'd have behaved just the same in his place."

Chapter Seven

Before I left the office that evening I had another session with Grant and we made final plans for the next day. I said I thought Clara and I ought to aim at reaching Castleton an hour or so before dusk so that we could locate Mam Tor and take a preliminary look at the approaches while there was still light enough to see—which meant arriving about a quarter to six. It was roughly a four-hour drive, so an early lunch and a start around half-past one seemed indicated. Grant agreed. It was decided that I should make all the arrangements with Clara, including fixing the place where I would pick her up. Grant confirmed that our rivals had agreed to call off their reporters until the results of our efforts were known, so we shouldn't have any difficulty in making an unnoticed departure, but he thought it would be wise for me to avoid Palmers Road all the same. Grant himself was going to attend to the money side. It seemed he'd had a talk that day with the Governor of the Bank, who had promised to have six thousand used five-pound notes discreetly packed in a strong suitcase and ready for collection at 12.30 p.m. the next day. Grant would pick up the case himself and would drive with it to a place called Henley's Corner, where the North Circular Road crossed my route out of town. He would be parked there from one-thirty onwards. I would pull up for a moment in front of him, take over the bag, and continue on my way.

Everything else was to be left entirely to me. Grant said he'd expect a call from me after the transfer, and that if he hadn't heard from me by midnight he'd assume something had gone seriously wrong and get the police on the job—though he didn't for a moment expect it would be necessary. He repeated that my sole task was to hand over the money and withdraw in good order with Clara. He warned me to be careful how I flashed my torch around in the presence of the kidnappers, so that they'd have no cause for alarm about identification. At the same time he said that anything I could pick up at the meeting might be useful afterwards, and that of course if I could get a line on where Landon would be released that would be a good thing, because though we were doing all this as a national service it *was* costing us thirty thousand pounds and he thought we were entitled to the exclusive story! At least he said it with a grin.

When I got home I rang Clara again. She'd had a talk with Barr and I gathered everything had been smoothed out and that she was now all set to leave. I told her I'd pick her up at the Marble Arch exit from Hyde Park at one-thirty precisely next day and that she'd better bring an overnight bag with her as we'd probably have to stay up north till the following morning. I said she'd better wear strong walking shoes, if she'd got any, as we might have to cover some rough ground. I also suggested it would be a good idea if she could make herself up to look as little like Clara Waugh as possible, since her face was now so well known to everyone, and she said she'd do her best. She sounded very excited.

By now I was beginning to feel pretty excited myself, and I had a restless night. I woke early, and by eight I'd dressed and breakfasted and packed everything I thought I'd need for the trip, including a powerful torch and a pair of binoculars. I was just going out to get the Riley filled up with petrol and oil when the phone rang. It was a bit early for calls and I thought it was probably Clara or Grant about the arrangements. But it wasn't. A cool voice said, "Hallo, Hugh—it's Mollie."

I said, "Well—hallo! This is a surprise."

"Is it? You know I promised to ring you."

"You're such an early bird."

"I wanted to be sure of getting you. . . . Look, I've got the day off—is there any chance you could take me out to lunch?"

I cursed inwardly. Of all the bad luck ...! But there wasn't anything I could do about it. I said, "Mollie, there's nothing I'd like better—but the fact is I've got a date already."

"Oh, dear ..." She sounded really disappointed. "Is it very important ...?"

"I'm afraid it is, rather."

"I *would* like to see you to-day ... You once said you'd break any date for me!"

"Unfortunately, this is work," I said. "I—I'm meeting a Belgian, a friend of the Editor's. I've got to tote him around."

"Too bad ... What about dinner, then?"

"I'm afraid I'll still have him on my hands."

"Well, come along to the flat when you're through—I'll make you some coffee."

"Taking chances, aren't you?"

"Perhaps I'm in the mood!"

This was getting worse and worse! "Look," I said desperately, "I know I'll be tied up with this man till midnight—can't we fix it for some other time? Tomorrow ...?"

"To-morrow *I'll* be busy," Mollie said. The friendliness had gone from her voice—she sounded like something left behind by the Ice Age. "It doesn't matter—it was just an idea ... Good-bye!" Abruptly, she rang off.

I felt very fed up. I'd half a mind to ring her back and try to pacify her, but I didn't see how I could without telling her more than she ought to know. I'd have to wait till the Landon affair was over, and then explain. She'd understand then. Still, it was damned annoying. ...

I was out of temper for quite a while, but I had things to do and the irritation gradually wore off. I got the car out, and had it fuelled, and then I drove to my favourite map shop in Long Acre. I couldn't rule out the possibility that somebody might be taking an interest, so just to be on the safe side I bought a whole lot of inch-to-the-mile maps and guide-books covering various parts of the country, including the Castleton area. Back at the flat, I read up all about Mam Tor in the Castleton guide-book. It was a small mountain in the High Peak district, its top about 1700 feet above sea-level, with a precipitous semi-circular edge on the Castleton side. It was known locally as the "Shivering Mountain"—apparently in frosty weather its shale and gritstone layers sometimes disintegrated, so that it gave the appearance of shivering. I hoped it wasn't an omen! Presently I turned to the inch-to-the-mile of the district. The nearest point to the mountain on the road was about a mile and a half to the west of Castleton. From there it would be about half a mile to the foot of the precipitous face. The road itself was over a thousand feet high, so I guessed the intervening ground would probably be rough moorland.

I put the map and guide-book in my bag, and cut some sandwiches and made a flask of coffee so that Clara and I wouldn't have to call in anywhere in the early evening. At noon I slipped out and had lunch in a pub that newspapermen didn't normally go to. Then, shortly after one, I put my bag in the Riley and set off through the thick traffic to the park. I was a little early, and stopped for a few minutes near Hyde Park Corner. It was exactly one-thirty when I reached Marble Arch. Clara was waiting just outside the gate—though if she hadn't seen me and waved I'd scarcely have recognised her. She was wearing low-heeled shoes and almost no make-up, and the difference was quite remarkable. Her hair, which she usually wore drawn back tight on one side in a rather sophisticated style, was now loose and girlish. She could have been anyone. She got quickly in beside me, and I drove off.

"Everything okay?" I said.

"I think so...." She sounded a bit tremulous. "That man rang me up again this morning."

"*Again!*"

"Yes—he said it was the last warning. He was threatening dreadful things if we—if we tried to bring the police in. He was horrible."

"Well, we're not going to, so I shouldn't let it disturb you.... When did he ring?"

"About ten."

"H'm—that means he'll have had plenty of time to get to Castleton before us if he wants to. Did he say anything else—apart from the threats?"

"No, he rang off practically at once. . . . That awful voice!—it gives me the creeps."

"Did you tell Ronald?"

"No, I thought I'd better not. . . . It wouldn't have taken much to upset him all over again. I told him everything was fine, and that I'd see him tomorrow. . . . Let's hope I was right!"

I concentrated on the traffic after that, with one eye on the clock. We were just about on schedule. We skirted Lords and joined the Finchley Road and ran through Golders Green and up past Temple Fortune. As we dropped down the slope on the other side I spotted Grant's grey Jaguar, drawn up on the near side just beyond the traffic lights. We were checked at the lights. Grant was looking round—he'd seen us. As the lights turned green I trickled across and pulled up ahead of the Jag. Grant was opening the car door. Nobody seemed to be paying any attention to us. I got out quickly and took the case from him. It was a brown fibre one, new and pretty heavy. The keys were tied to the handle. Grant gave me a conspiratorial grin. "Everything all right?" he asked. I nodded. "Good luck, then—I'll expect to hear from you tonight." He waved to Clara. I slung the case in the back of the Riley, and drove on.

The first hurdle was behind us, anyway!

Chapter Eight

I was very much aware of all those notes in the back and I kept a sharp look-out for possible trouble, both ahead and in the driving mirror. There'd been too much gossip about me and the money for me to feel entirely comfortable. Many a hi-jacking job had been staged for a fraction of what was in that suitcase, and if the talk in the Fleet Street pubs had happened to reach the underworld it wasn't beyond the bounds of possibility that an eye had been kept on me. But it was only a precautionary thought, and I wasn't really worried.

Actually, my first anxiety was of quite another sort. There was a fair amount of traffic on the stretch of road after Barnet, and as I wasn't hurrying, most of the stuff going my way was passing me. But after a while I noticed that one car—a black Wolseley—was keeping its place behind me all the time, and only about fifty yards away. I slowed a little, and it slowed too. I accelerated to sixty and left it behind, but in a few moments it had caught up again. It had no aerial or police sign, but I could see a uniformed man behind the wheel and another one beside him and I was pretty sure they were police. I didn't say anything to Clara, but I kept watching. They *shouldn't* have been following me, even to give protection—not after the guarantee of non-interference the *Record* had been given. . . . Suddenly, a nasty suspicion entered my mind. Had I, perhaps, been a little too innocent in accepting Grant's assurances at their face value? Was it possible, in spite of all the pledges, that we *were* secretly playing in with the authorities—that there *was* going to be a trap . . .? Yet the police surely wouldn't have used uniformed men to follow me?—that would have been crazy. Anyway, I didn't think Grant would do that to me. It was an unworthy thought—but I continued to keep an eye on the car. Then, at Potters Bar, it turned off, and that was that.

Presently, Clara began to talk to me. Until now she'd always struck me as a rather intense, smouldering sort of person—with explosive possibilities, I suspected, but hardly vivacious. However, I'd only seen her under the worst conditions. Now that she had a real hope her father might be freed, she was much more lively and cheerful. She asked me how long I'd been on the *Record*, and if I enjoyed being a reporter, and I told her a bit about the life as we cruised along. She asked me if I had many jobs to do that were as exciting as this one, and I said that happily I didn't.

There was a little pause then. I was curious about *her*, too. I couldn't forget the things Lawson had said about her, and I wondered how much truth there'd been in his account. After a moment I said, "How do you like being an actress?"

She made a deprecatory sound. "I'm not much of an actress, I'm afraid. I'm not much of anything, really. . . ."

"Oh, come!"

"It's true . . . I was a frightful flop at drama school. I get a booking occasionally, but it never amounts to anything much. I call myself an actress because it sounds better but that's not how I earn my living—when I do earn one! I'm really a model."

"You mean you—wear clothes?"

She gave a wry sort of smile. "Very much the reverse!"

"Oh, I see—that sort of model. . . . Well, I suppose you don't mind it?"

"I don't specially like it—but it's something I can do."

"What does your father think about it?"

"Not much."

"Perhaps he'd have preferred you to be a physicist!"

"He'd have preferred me to keep house for him, actually, but I'm hopeless at domestic things."

We broke off while I manœuvred my way past a convoy of lorries. Then I said, "You're not very like your father, are you?—not like the photographs I've seen, anyway."

"No, I'm not a bit like him. I'm exactly like my mother—or so he always says. She was Italian, you know."

"Yes, I heard that.... She must have been very lovely."

"Thank you...! I don't actually remember much about her—she died when I was quite small. Father was absolutely devoted to her, I know that. She was a gay, vital, temperamental person—really just the opposite of him. He worshipped her...." Her voice trailed off.

I said, "Are you very fond of your father?"

"Well—yes. He's—he's a wonderful man."

"Is he fond of you?"

"Very."

"It seems odd that you didn't see more of each other."

I felt her swivel round to stare at me. "What makes you say that?"

"Oh, I heard someone talking—another reporter. He knew one of the scientists at Crede, and apparently this chap had said your father had been complaining because he hadn't had a chance to see you for eight months."

The engine suddenly seemed very noisy. I almost wished I hadn't said it—her relations with her father weren't really my business. And yet, in a way, they were, because she *had* been less than frank at that conference. I wondered what she'd say now.

She said, in a very subdued voice, "Actually, that's true."

"Is it ...? At the Ministry, you said you hadn't seen him for 'a month or two.' "

"I know—I just didn't want to have to explain...." There was another pause.

"Anyway, it's nothing to do with me," I said.

"No, it isn't—but I don't mind telling you. In fact, I'd like to."

I waited.

"The truth is," she said, "I *wasn't* on very good terms with my father—though I am now. It's the old story—I wanted to live my own life, and he didn't like the way I was going about it. We looked at everything differently. He's rather an ascetic and I'm just the opposite. His idea of enjoying himself is to get on with his work.

I'm afraid mine was quite different. As soon as I could I got away on my own. I wanted to have a fling. When I was just twenty-one I married a man I met at a party. I married him two days after the party. I thought I was terribly in love with him. Father was horrified, because I really didn't know anything about the man. As it turned out, Father was right. The marriage was an utter disaster from the very beginning. I ought to have made it up with him then, but I didn't. I felt I didn't care what happened. I had a few affairs, and I drank a lot, and I got in with some pretty frightful people. Father found out what was happening, and he came up and we had rows—but the more fuss he made the more determined I was to go my own way. I was an utter fool—and I wrote some beastly things to him. . . ." She broke off. She seemed to be in great distress.

I said, "Look, I wish I hadn't brought it up. You don't have to tell me."

"I've told you the worst," she said. "After that, things suddenly got better. I met Ronald. Ronald did something to me. You only know him as a rather angry man, but actually he's terribly kind and gentle. About the first thing he wanted to do was meet my father, so I wrote to Crede and of course Father came like a shot. *That* was the first time we'd met for eight months. Father liked Ronald at once—they got on splendidly. After that it was easy. Father and I became friends again. We were wonderfully happy—for about three weeks. Then this ghastly thing had to happen to him. When I think how much I hurt him, how badly I treated him, I can hardly bear it. . . . It's hell to feel remorse when you know it may be too late."

"Let's hope it won't be," I said.

She nodded. The tears were flowing unchecked down her cheeks. I watched the road. It was extraordinary, I thought, how right Lawson had been about her in some ways, and yet how completely wrong in others. I could well understand why she hadn't wanted to say all that in public. . . . Presently she dried her eyes and began to powder her face. By the time we reached Welwyn she was back to normal.

We were just leaving Bedford when I first noticed the grey car on my tail. At least, that was when I became conscious of it—I had an idea I'd seen it before, a long way back, but I'd been talking then and I hadn't bothered. Now I did. We were cruising at a fairly steady fifty. The grey car was keeping about a quarter of a mile behind, but I noticed that it closed up through villages and whenever the road started to wind. I thought there was only one person in it, but I couldn't be sure. It was a newish-looking car, with a lot of chromium. I told myself I was imagining things, but it seemed better to make sure, all the same. I slowed to thirty. A couple of cars rushed by, but neither of them was the grey one. I slowed still further, and it still didn't pass me. The distance between us was about the same.

Clara said, "What's the matter?"

"There's a car behind that I can't shake off . . . I think it's following us."

She turned in alarm, gazing through the rear window. For a moment she watched in silence. Then she said, "Oughtn't we to stop and make sure?"

I was wondering about that. I said, "If it *is* following us, it's probably the man who rang you this morning—the kidnapper. I don't see who else it can be. And if it's the kidnapper, I suppose we ought to ignore him. Our rendezvous is on Mam Tor, not A.5."

"Suppose it's not the kidnapper—it could be terribly dangerous. . . ."

"Yes, that's just it. . . ."

"If you drove faster perhaps you could leave him behind."

"We'll try," I said. "Hold on to your seat."

I opened up the Riley, and in a few seconds we were doing well over seventy. I passed the two cars that had just passed me, and got some ugly looks. The road was fairly clear and I stepped hard on the gas, pushing the needle up to eighty in places. Then there was a road-up sign, and a bit of a block, and afterwards there was a winding stretch that slowed me, and quite a lot of traffic. All the same, we covered ten miles at a pretty fast pace. Then, on a straight stretch, I looked in the mirror and saw that the grey car was still on my tail. There was no doubt about it now—we *were* being followed.

"I do think we ought to stop," Clara said again. She'd turned to take another look at the car. "I doubt if it is the kidnapper—I'm sure he'd never risk showing himself to us in daylight."

She had a point there. It didn't seem very likely.

Suddenly, out of the blue, she said, "You know, it looks a bit like Ronald's car!"

I nearly shot out of my seat. I remembered now that Barr *had* had a grey car. I said, "What is his car?"

She frowned. "I think he said it was a Zephyr. It's a new one."

I looked at the grey car again in the driving mirror. It was too far away for me to be certain, but it could have been a Zephyr.

I said, "*Surely* he wouldn't have followed us—not after he'd agreed to keep out of it? Not after everything was settled?"

"I can't believe he would either," Clara said. She looked as worried as I felt. "But he's very stubborn, he might have done.... What are you going to do?"

"I think you're right—we'll have to stop and make sure."

I drove on till I came to a lay-by in the middle of a mile-straight stretch. There was a lorry there, with a couple of tough-looking chaps standing talking beside it. I turned and parked behind it. The grey car was about four hundred yards away. Suddenly it pulled in to the side of the road and stopped. I got the binoculars from my bag and focused them on it. I couldn't see the driver's face because the windscreen was reflecting like a mirror—but the car *was* a Zephyr, a new one.

"The stupid idiot!" I said savagely.

Clara bit her lip. "Shall I walk back? Perhaps I can make him see reason."

"If you couldn't before," I said, "you probably can't now."

"Well, if you think he'll pay more attention to you...."

I hesitated. I wasn't keen on leaving Clara alone there with thirty thousand pounds, even for a few minutes. I wasn't sure I'd do any good, either. If Barr had disregarded the arguments of yesterday, I couldn't see why he should be persuaded to-day. Perhaps if I drove flat out I'd be able to lose him in time—get far enough ahead to take a side turning anyway, and give him the slip. . . . But there was a lot of traffic about, and the very last thing we wanted was any kind of mishap, or trouble with the police. . . . Better, perhaps, to have a show-down. But not here. Somewhere where we could all join in.

I told Clara what I was going to do. Then I started the engine and pulled out into the road again. The Zephyr followed. I finished the straight mile at speed and entered a village with a thirty-mile limit. The road curved in the middle of it. Just beyond the bend there was a cobbled parking place on the near side. I pulled in and stopped. In a few moments the grey car came cautiously round the corner. The driver was looking around, examining the parked cars before going on. . . .

I could hardly believe my eyes. It wasn't Ronald Barr. It was Mollie!

Chapter Nine

She saw me, and braked. Then, quite coolly, she reversed and drew in alongside us, winding her nearside window down. "Well," she said, with a faint smile, "we meet again. . . . Your Belgian, I presume!"

I was so angry with her, I could scarcely speak. It was obvious, now, that her morning call had merely been to check up that I was going to be out of town, that I was taking the money that day—and I deeply resented the trick. Also, I could see stacks of trouble ahead.

I got out of the car and walked round to her. "Just what is the idea?" I said.

"I'd have thought that was obvious—I'm following you. I've followed you all the way from Chancery Lane. It's been quite difficult, I can tell you."

"You'd no right to."

"Oh? Why not? You've followed me often enough." Her composure was infuriating. "Didn't you once tell me it was a standing instruction at the *Record*—'keep your eye on Mollie'? Well, now I'm keeping my eye on Hugh! It's only fair."

Clara called, "Who is it, Hugh?" She obviously didn't remember Mollie. Her face was pale with anxiety.

"Another reporter," I told her. "Mollie Bourne, of the *Courier*."

Mollie said, "So it's 'Hugh' now, is it? My, you are on good terms!"

"Look, Mollie," I said, "this isn't an ordinary story. . . ."

"It certainly isn't. . . ." She gave Clara a cold stare. "It looks more like a promising elopement to me. Everything so cosy, and thirty thousand pounds in the back of the car!"

"Mollie, this isn't a joking matter—it's serious. . . . You've no

77

right to be here. The *Courier's* agreed not to interfere—everyone has."

"*I* haven't," she said. " And I've got the day off—I told you. I've got to-morrow off, too!"

"If the *Courier* hears about it, they'll be mad."

She gave me her "spoiled darling" look. "That I rather doubt—especially if I go back with an exciting story of how the money was handed over, and perhaps even an interview with Arthur Landon. They're very forgiving at the *Courier*."

I said, "Listen, Mollie—we've been warned that if anyone else is seen around at the rendezvous, Landon will be killed. I think he will be. Surely you don't want to put a man's life in danger for the sake of a story?"

"I shan't put anyone's life in danger if I keep in the background. . . ."

"There won't be any background. They'll be watching every move we make from the time we get there. For all we know, they may be watching us at this very moment."

"It seems most unlikely," Mollie said. She was quite unmoved.

Clara had left the Riley and joined us. Her face was white. "*Please*, Miss Bourne!" she said. "Please leave us alone. My father's in terrible danger already. . . . *Don't* make it worse."

Mollie ignored her. I wouldn't have believed she could have behaved so badly. "Where's the rendezvous?" she asked me.

"I wouldn't dream of telling you."

"Then I shall keep right behind you. I can, you know—this car goes awfully well. The hire people had just tuned it. It's not quite as fast as the Sunbeam Talbot, but it's much less conspicuous, don't you think . . .? Well—shall we go?"

I looked at the Zephyr, new and zippy, and I looked at Mollie. She was one of the finest drivers I'd ever known—I'd chased her up hill and down dale too often to have any doubts about that. I'd already made one attempt to shake her off that day, and it hadn't worked. Now that there was nothing to stop her keeping close behind me, I wouldn't have a hope.

I played my last card. "All right," I said, "if you won't leave us alone we can't go through with it, that's all.... We shall turn back."

Clara cried, "But, Hugh, we *can't*...."

"We've no choice. If we can't keep to the conditions, it's safer not to show up at all."

"But they'll kill him ...!"

"They may wait to find out what's happened. I'll ring up Grant and ask him to put something in tomorrow's paper—he could say that things went wrong and that we'll have another try later. Honestly, Clara, it's much better than going on...."

Clara turned on Mollie, her eyes blazing. "How *can* you do this ...? It doesn't mean a thing to you—it means everything to me. Haven't you any heart at all? What sort of a woman are you?"

"I'm a newspaperwoman, "Mollie said coldly.

Clara took a quick step forward. She was tense with fury and looked as though she was going to tear Mollie apart. "You're a bitch!—a bloody little bitch!"

Mollie looked at me and gave a faint shrug.

I said, "All the same, she's not far out, Mollie. I just don't know what's got into you. You *are* being heartless—and damned irresponsible, too. You know what Landon's safety means. I can't imagine what you think you're playing at.... Well, am I to turn round?"

Mollie was pale now, too. For a moment she hesitated. Then she said, "I might do a deal with you."

"What sort of deal?"

"You tell me the name of the last place you'll be passing through before you reach your destination. Then you can go on alone. I'll follow later, and put up at the place for the night. After you've handed over the money, you'll come and tell me what happened before you send anything."

"Why, it's practically blackmail! Of all the unscrupulous ...!"

"Did I ever say I was scrupulous?"

I glanced at Clara. The tense look had gone from her face. She was obviously considering the offer. After a moment she said, "That ought to be safe enough, Hugh—as long as we can trust her."

It certainly seemed the best we could hope for. I turned to Mollie again. "Do you promise you'll stay put at this place, and not try to follow us?"

"Yes—as long as you promise to come and see me immediately afterwards. But if you cheat, I swear I'll never speak to you again."

"The same goes for me," I said. "Frankly, I'm not sure I want to anyway. . . . All right, it's a deal. The last place is Castleton, in Derbyshire, and there's a pub there called the George. I'll see you there at about ten to-night."

Mollie nodded. "Look after yourself," she said.

Clara had already turned towards the Riley. I joined her, and a moment later we drove off.

Chapter Ten

The incident weighed on me. I knew from experience that Mollie took a lot of putting off once she was on the trail of a good story, but at least it was usually her own story. Also, though she valued her success and her reputation, I'd never known her ride roughshod over people's deepest feelings and interests to get what she wanted, the way she just had. To me, she'd been almost unrecognisable. I felt very troubled, and drove in a brooding silence. It was Clara who spoke first.

"You know Miss Bourne pretty well, don't you?" she said.

"Very well."

"And you like her?"

"Normally I like her a lot."

There was a little pause. Then Clara said, "I shouldn't have called her names. It was very rude. I'm afraid I lost my temper."

"I don't blame you," I said. "Let's not talk about it."

We saw no more of Mollie, and there were no further incidents. We by-passed Derby and continued along A.6 through Matlock, and by half-past five we were running into Castleton. It was much as I remembered it—a pleasantly-situated, grey stone village, with a lot of tourist signs—though on this March weekday it was almost deserted. I drove straight through it and out on the road towards Chapel-en-le-Frith, climbing steeply to a hairpin bend that gave us our first sight of the rounded top of Mam Tor. From the height we were already at it didn't look much of a mountain, but the eastern face, rising almost sheer for several hundred feet, was impressive. I pulled the car off the road and got the binoculars out again. The foot of the precipice was hidden from the road by high grassy hummocks, so we climbed the shoulder of the hill to get a better view. There had been a shower that day and the ground had a surface dampness, but a long dry spell had caked it hard underneath and the going was easy. Soon I was able to study the place that the kidnappers had appointed for the meeting. I could just make out the fallen notice board, lying at the foot of the cliff at a point where the drop was rather less high than in the centre. As I'd expected, the ground between the road and the fence was uncultivated moorland, unfenced and quite easy to negotiate in daylight. At night it would be rough going because of the hummocks—but we'd manage. The whole place had a wild and desolate air about it, which the occasional passing car did little to relieve. I wondered if we ourselves were being observed from some point up on the mountain or on the high moors opposite, and thought it most likely. Since we'd nothing to hide, it was probably better that we should be. We continued to reconnoitre for a while. I made a mental note of the best way through the hummocks, so that we'd have less difficulty after dark. Then we got back into the car and I drove on for a mile or two and found a quiet spot well away from Mam Tor where we could eat our sandwiches and drink our coffee.

We'd not yet had a look inside the suitcase, and this seemed to be the moment. I unlocked it and opened the lid and there the money was—a fascinating sight. It was done up in bundles of a hundred notes, each with an elastic band round it. I delved a bit, and checked that they were all well-used notes. I went through one bundle, and there were definitely no signs of any marks. Everything was above board. I locked up the case again, and we settled down to wait.

The time passed slowly. Now that we were so near the moment of transfer, tension filled the car. Seeing all that money had made me much more aware of the risks we were taking. The stake was far too high for comfort. The thought that we would soon be face to face with criminals who had dared to seize and hide a man, and coolly bargain over his life or death, wasn't at all pleasant. As darkness fell, the strain grew greater. We sat and smoked, and from time to time made an effort to talk, but mostly we just listened to the moaning wind and watched the clock. Seven-thirty, I'd decided, would be our zero hour.

The moment came at last. I started the engine and drove slowly back to the point opposite the precipice and parked the car off the road with the lights off. I slipped a heavy spanner into my raincoat pocket, found the torch, and got out the suitcase. A car swept by with lights blazing and quickly disappeared. For a second or two we stood listening. We seemed to be quite alone. The night was very dark. I said, "Right—let's get this over," and picked up the suitcase and started off towards the face of the Shivering Mountain, with Clara close behind me.

It was an awkward as well as a nerve-racking journey. In spite of my careful reconnaissance we were soon lost among the hummocks, and the ground was even rougher than I'd thought. Although I used the torch freely, one or other of us kept stumbling over small bits of rock or slipping into the trickling streams. The suitcase was heavy, and I had no free hand to help Clara. Once, as she tripped and clutched my arm for support, I felt her trembling. She was forcing herself to keep going, I knew, only by a great effort—but she didn't hesitate, and we plodded on. Presently the hummocks began to flatten out, and we emerged into a shallow basin at the foot of the cliff. We were almost there. It was two minutes to eight by my watch as we approached the precipice. I shone the torch around and picked out the broken notice board. The words on it were still legible—DANGER, FALLING STONES. For us, I thought, that was probably the least of the dangers!

Eight o'clock! We were right on time. Now that we'd reached the place, I couldn't help feeling surprised at the kidnappers' choice of a rendezvous. It was so completely shut-in that it would have made the perfect trap, if we'd intended a trap. I wondered if they were already there, waiting and watching in the darkness, or whether they were coming up behind us. We listened, but except for the soughing of the wind there wasn't a sound. I swung the torch beam round like a searchlight, but there was nothing to be seen except boulders and sedge grass and the red-brown face of the cliff.

Five-past eight! Clara said, in a low, strained voice, "I wonder what's happened to them." I was beginning to get worried, too. It would be a fine thing if they'd taken fright after all this and decided not to keep the appointment. Yet their instructions had been followed implicitly and I couldn't imagine why they should have changed their plans—not with the thirty thousand pounds practically within their grasp. Perhaps they'd been delayed. . . .

At that moment I heard a sound above us, and a few small stones spattered at our feet. I pulled Clara away from the face and shone the torch upwards. The sound grew louder—a curious slithering, very high up and almost exactly above our heads. For an incredulous moment I thought that someone was being lowered down the precipice on a rope. More pieces of shale showered down. There *was* someone up there. Something, anyway. I searched the face with the torch beam. The sound was getting closer. Suddenly I drew in my breath sharply as the light caught something in motion. A rope *was* being lowered from the top—though not with anyone on it. The loose end was tied round a piece of rock, that was all. It was coming down quite fast, dislodging bits of debris in its passage. As it reached eye-level I grabbed it. There was a sheet of paper tucked between the rope and the stone. I slipped it out. There was something thin and round inside it—a pencil. Together, Clara and I bent over the paper. There was a message on it, in the usual newspaper capitals. It said:

TIE THE CASE SECURELY TO THE ROPE. THAT IS ALL. IF THE MONEY IS FOUND TO BE IN ORDER LANDON WILL BE RELEASED TO-MORROW NIGHT. WRITE ON THE PAPER WHERE MRS. WAUGH WILL BE STAYING. LANDON WILL JOIN HER THERE ABOUT 10 P.M.

I slid the stone out, and hauled on the rope till I had plenty of slack, and passed the end round the case, with a couple of turns round the handle, and made it fast. It was clear now why the kidnappers had insisted on a strong case! Then I wrote on the

84

paper, "Mrs. Waugh will be at the George Hotel, Castleton," and slipped the paper under the tied rope, and gave a tug. Whoever was at the top seemed to test the rope for strain, and then the case went slowly up and out of sight. There were more showers of debris, heavier now, as the case bumped and banged against the face. They continued for a couple of minutes. Then all was silence again.

I had to help Clara back to the car. Reaction had set in, and she suddenly seemed drained of strength. To me, the episode had been very much of an anti-climax—though I wasn't complaining. I was thankful it had happened that way. I certainly had to hand it to the kidnappers. It had been a brilliantly devised plan for the transfer, and a most efficient bit of execution. They'd taken no serious risks at all. Even if Clara and I *had* been working with the police in an effort to trap them, they'd have had a good chance of getting clear away before anyone could have worked round the precipice face and climbed to the top. They'd played it safe all through—and right to the end they hadn't shown themselves to anybody. That gave me confidence that Clara's troubles would soon be over, and I told her so. For the first time, I really believed that Landon would be freed.

It took us half an hour to get back to the car and clean up, and it was after nine when we checked in at the George. Mollie's Zephyr was in the drive, but I couldn't see any sign of Mollie herself. Clara registered as Laura Brown. Landon wasn't safe yet, and I didn't want anyone to know his daughter was in the district until he was actually free. She got one or two curious glances from the staff, I thought, but no one appeared to recognise her.

Dinner was officially over, but the proprietress said we could have some cold chicken and salad. While it was being prepared we went into the bar and Clara knocked back three large pink gins in the time it took me to sink a pint of beer. After a day on the wagon she was obviously alcohol-starved. She revived considerably with the third one, and wanted to ring up her fiancé and tell him what had happened. I thought she'd drunk too much for discretion on the telephone and tried to dissuade her. I said the

Editor would ring Barr later and set his mind at rest and that that was the safer way. She began to get tearful—but then, fortunately, we were called to eat. By the time we'd finished the meal she was sagging again with tiredness and soon afterwards she went up to her room. I wasn't sorry to have her off my hands. One way and another, it had been quite a day!

I was on my way to ring Grant when I ran into Mollie in the hall. She'd just come in from a stroll. Her face, I thought, showed relief when she saw me. Anyway, she gave me a very warm smile. "Well, how did it go?" she asked.

"All right, thank you," I said stiffly. Now that the worst of the danger was over my resentment had faded a little, but I still couldn't quite forgive her for the way she'd behaved.

"Where's your girl friend?"

"She's gone to bed."

"Good! So what happened?"

I told her about the rendezvous, and the message, and the kidnappers' promise that Landon would be released next day. I kept it brief—there wasn't really very much to say. She listened with absorbed interest to the end.

"That's it, then," I said. "Now I hope you're satisfied!"

She looked at me oddly. "Why should I be satisfied?"

"Well, you've got the story, such as it is. . . . And as you said, if you stick around and we're lucky you may even be able to muscle in on the Landon interview."

She said, "You don't really suppose I came all the way up here to get that, do you?"

"Of course."

"Then you're an ass! The *Record's* virtually bought the story, hasn't it? If Landon is released, you'll obviously get a jolly good scoop, which you'll have paid for. You don't imagine I'd want to send the *Courier* a few miserable scraps from the rich man's table?"

I stared at her in astonishment. "Then why in heaven's name *did* you come?"

"I just thought I'd like to be around!" she said. She smiled again, sweetly. "Good night, Hugh!—sleep well!"

Chapter Eleven

I rang the office and was put straight through to Grant. He sounded most relieved to hear from me. I told him, without going into details on the phone, that the mission had been successfully completed, that there had been no direct contact with "our friends," but that if they kept their renewed promises I ought to be meeting the man we wanted to interview in about twenty-four hours and that I was staying on for that purpose. He said, "Fine!—I'll be looking forward to another call from you to-morrow night." I asked him if he'd tell Barr that all was well, and he said he would, and after a final "Good luck!" he rang off.

I slept like a log that night and woke in the morning feeling refreshed and ready for anything. It was just as well I did, because with Mollie and Clara both around and no other visible guests in the hotel I could see the atmosphere was going to be pretty strained. I'd hoped at least to get breakfast over on my own, but both girls came down before I'd finished. Clara joined me. Once again she hadn't made up much, and her face showed the ravages of a restless night. Mollie ate alone at the other side of the dining-room. She couldn't have been more distant and disapproving if she'd caught Clara and me on an illicit week-end. It baffled me why she was sticking around.

Talking to Clara wasn't at all easy. She was terribly on edge, and naturally she couldn't think of anything except whether her father would turn up or not. I gave her all the encouragement I could, but my assurances sounded pretty empty, even to me. The night was going to bring tragedy or happiness for her but there was no means of knowing which and her guess was as good as mine. I asked her if she'd like me to drive her round the Derbyshire beauty spots to take her mind off things, but she said she wasn't fit company—which was true enough—and that she'd sooner stay in and rest. For a while after breakfast she hung about listlessly. Then she said she was going back to her room. I said would it be all right with her if I went out for the day and she said of course it would and she'd see me in the evening.

Mollie's car was still in the drive but she was nowhere to be seen. It looked as though she'd gone to ground, too. I debated whether to go in search of her, and decided not to. As things were, we'd probably only have a row. I read through the papers, and then set off in the car to explore some of the Peak country. It was a fine spring day and very pleasant out—though judging by the way the barometer had plunged when I'd tapped it that morning, we were in for a change. I lunched at Matlock, and walked all afternoon through a beautiful dale called the Lathkill, and got back to Castleton about half-past five. Clara had just had tea and was sitting in the lounge. I asked her how she'd been getting on and she said it had been a fairly grim day but she'd been better on her own and had had a good rest. She'd lunched in her room, I gathered, and hadn't seen anything of Mollie. She asked me if I'd had an enjoyable day, and I enthused for a while about the Lathkill.

"I think perhaps *I'd* better go for a walk before dinner," she said. "It's that or the bar—and I wouldn't want Father to find me quite tight when he arrives!" She got up. I saw that she'd already changed into walking shoes.

"Would you like me to come with you?" I asked.

"No, don't bother—I'm sure you must have had all the walking you want for one day. . . . And I'd really sooner be alone."

I nodded. "Don't get wet—I think it's going to rain."

"I'll watch it," she said. She gave me a pallid smile, and went out. I walked over to the window. The sun was just dipping behind a nasty-looking cloudbank low on the horizon. I heard the front door bang, and watched Clara as she walked briskly down towards the road. A moment later I heard the door bang again. This time it was Mollie, in a smart raincoat. She had something tucked under her arm—it looked to me like a torch. She, too, walked briskly down the drive. She stopped at the gate, glanced cautiously up and down the road, and then set off in the same direction as Clara. For a moment, I hesitated. Then I picked up my coat and went after her. By the time I caught her up we were leaving the village. Clara had disappeared round a bend ahead.

Mollie turned at the sound of my step. She looked surprised, but not particularly annoyed. "Now who's following who?" she said.

I fell in beside her. "*You're* following Clara."

"Perhaps."

"Why, for heaven's sake? She's only going for a walk before dinner."

"Perhaps."

I said, "I don't get it at all. You've obviously got it in for her, but I don't know why. She's done nothing to you."

"I've got a hunch," Mollie said.

"What sort of hunch?"

"I just don't think Clara's quite what she seems to be. . . . I never have thought so." She quickened her step a little as we turned the corner. Clara was just disappearing out of sight again. Dusk was beginning to fall.

I said, "I wish you'd tell me why. I'm not trying to pinch a story or anything—but you've been going on in such a strange way I really would like to get things straight. . . . What makes you so suspicious?"

"Well, I'll tell you. . . . Do you remember an incident after that first Press conference, when we were standing out in the street and Ronald Barr was kissing Clara good-bye?"

"I remember. You looked as though you'd seen a ghost."

"I'd certainly seen something that wasn't natural. Clara's face was turned away from you, and towards me. When Barr bent to kiss her, she positively flinched. She had an expression of absolute revulsion!"

It seemed scarcely possible. I said, "Are you sure you weren't imagining things?"

"I'm dead sure. Clara looked just as though she was being given the kiss of death."

"But, Mollie, she's terribly fond of him. She was telling me about him on the way up. She said the nicest things about him."

"That doesn't mean she's fond of him. It only means she wanted you to think so."

"Why should she? Supposing you're right—what does it prove?"

"I don't know what it proves. All I know is that it's interesting. There's something phony going on, and I'd like to know what."

"And *that's* why you came all the way up here?"

"A hunch is a hunch!—and I had two days off. Judging by what's happened, I think the trip's been justified."

"What do you mean?"

"Well, there's been some odd behaviour. . . ."

"By you, yes!"

"Not just by me. . . . Why do you think the kidnappers are letting Landon come to Castleton?"

I shrugged. "If they've been hiding him around here and they knew Clara was in the district it was the obvious thing to do, wasn't it?"

"You mean they were being human and considerate?"

"I suppose so."

"Why should they bother? They certainly haven't been very considerate up to now. . . . I'd have thought that once they'd got their money they'd have freed Landon and let him make his own way home—not worried about arranging for his reception."

I said, "It's a point, of course. . . . Why do *you* think they made the arrangement, then?"

"The only thing I can think of is that they might have wanted to give Clara an excuse for staying up here."

I was still baffled. "Why should she want to stay up here?"

"I don't know," Mollie said. "That's why I've been keeping an eye on her all day. That's why I'm following her now!"

It made no sense at all to me. If Clara was a phony, I couldn't imagine what she was being a phony about, or why. All the same, her present behaviour was beginning to puzzle me. As we rounded yet another bend, I saw that she'd left the road and struck off up a track to the left. It led, if my recollection of the inch-to-the-mile was right, to nowhere at all except wild and open moorland. An excellent place for a walk in daylight—but by now it was nearly dark. . . . In the end I stopped searching for explanations and concentrated on keeping her in sight without being seen.

For a while it was simple. Though we were climbing slowly to a high plateau, the ground was undulating and gave us good cover. The dusk was in our favour. But then, as it deepened into darkness, we had to close in, moving cautiously and stopping frequently to locate by sound what we couldn't see. For a time there *were* sounds—faint, but adequate. Clara was walking fast, and every few minutes we caught the click of a heel against stone. Then the surface of the ground grew softer, and the track seemed to divide, and while we were listening and debating which way to go we lost her. The last thing I heard was a faint sound over my right shoulder, as though she'd made a half-circle and turned for home. Then silence fell.

"Well, that's that," I said. "She's obviously going back to the hotel. . . . So much for hunches!"

Mollie said, "Who'd walk up here for fun in the dark—alone?"

"It needn't have been for fun," I said. "It could have been out of sheer fed-upness. When you're desperately worried, this kind of place appeals. Suits the mood!"

Mollie said nothing. Instead, she switched her torch on and continued slowly along the track. It was partly made up, as though it had been used for carts at some time. Other tracks ran off in all directions. Mollie chose one of them at random. I said, "At this rate we'll probably lose ourselves as well as Clara!" I made a mental note that the sunset glow had been on our right coming up and that the sky in the west was still a little lighter than the rest. I held my watch in the torch beam. "It's a quarter past seven. Why don't we go back and have a drink before dinner?"

Mollie stopped. "I suppose that is the only thing to do," she said. But she sounded reluctant to leave the place. She swivelled the torch around—and suddenly, with an exclamation, she bent-down. There was a footmark in the black, peaty soil of the track, with a very clear, heavily-ribbed pattern. It was a large print—certainly not Clara's. A man's. There were more of them, pointing ahead of us.

I said, "Probably just a shepherd." I was beginning to feel I could use that drink.

"I don't believe shepherds wear shoes like that," Mollie said.

"A walker, then. These moors are a hiker's paradise."

"There wouldn't be many people around on a weekday in March," Mollie said.

"They may be old prints."

"They look pretty fresh to me. . . . Let's see where they lead."

She moved on. For a few yards we followed the tracks easily. Then they disappeared as the path became stony. We were going gently downhill now. I had the impression we were entering a shallow valley with higher ground all round. I was about to say that now we'd lost the tracks we might just as well turn back when Mollie, who was leading with the torch, stopped abruptly. "Look!" she said, shining the light straight down.

I looked. I thought from her tone she'd found something exciting, but I was disappointed. It was only a hole in the ground, and not a big one. The opening was scarcely more than two feet across. It lay just off the path. I dropped a stone down and it reached the bottom almost at once. The hole was only about six feet deep. "It's a tiny pothole," I said. "What they call a swallow. This is limestone country—they're all over the place."

Mollie had bent down and was shining the torch right into the hole. She held the light there so long that I grew impatient. "What on earth can you see?" I asked.

She got up slowly and gave me the torch. "Well," she said, in a voice that suddenly seemed not quite under control, "we may have lost Clara but we've found something else. Take a look!"

I knelt down and thrust the torch at arm's length into the hole. It was a little out of plumb, but I could see the bottom well enough. There was a muddy floor, churned up by feet and showing many marks. Some of the marks were of heavily ribbed shoes. But that wasn't all. A little to the left, on a ledge of earth, there were four shallow, triangular indentations, the corners of a rectangle about two feet long and nine inches wide. I didn't need telling what they were. Someone had rested a heavy suitcase there!

Chapter Twelve

There was no question of piecing things together at that stage. I was so astounded by our discovery that I found it difficult to think at all. I couldn't believe it was entirely by chance that we'd come upon the pothole after following Clara, and to that extent I accepted Mollie's hunch about her—but I was still nowhere near guessing what she'd been up to. As far as the hole itself was concerned I thought merely that it had been used by the kidnappers as a temporary hiding place for the money. Even so, it seemed worth while to go down and take a closer look. I got Mollie to hold the torch and lowered myself carefully into the swallow. It was a fairly tight squeeze getting through, but the jagged, yellowish-white sides had plenty of handy projections and in no time at all I was standing beside the suitcase marks. Mollie passed the torch down to me and I flashed it around. At once, the picture changed dramatically. The sides of the hole widened out like a flask at the bottom, and I saw with a thrill of excitement that on one side a low passage led out of it. I called up to Mollie, "There's more in this place than meets the eye—you'd better come down!" She was in the hole almost before I'd got the words out. I took her weight, and helped her down, and in a moment she was standing beside me, gazing with awed enthusiasm at the low passage.

I crouched down and shone the torch into it. It was only about three feet high at the entrance but it opened out almost at once into what appeared to be a small cave. On the floor of the cave, to the right, there was something that looked like the end of a pick handle. There must be a recess there, that I couldn't see into. I crawled through, with Mollie at my heels. The torch beam lit up a row of sleeping bats hanging from the roof. Big cave spiders darted away from the glare. The cave was about ten feet in diameter. I flashed the torch into the recess. The wooden handle I'd seen was part of a small sledgehammer. There was a lot of other equipment there—a stack of iron pistons with rings at the top; a box of tinned food; a box of magnesium flares; a steel helmet, rather like a coal-miner's, with a lamp in the front; a boiler-suit of thick grey canvas; a leather belt with a flat electric lamp attached to it; and a lot of spare batteries. The cave was obviously a store. More than that, though—a staging post. At the far side the passage continued, but higher and wider, sloping down between rough walls of mountain limestone into the unknown depths.

I looked at Mollie. Her eyes were shining, and it wasn't just the reflection of the light. I said, "Well, we seem to be on to something big. The question is, what do we do?"

"Keep going," Mollie said. "Landon could be here. It would be a wonderful place to hide anybody."

"He could be," I agreed. "So could the kidnappers!"

"I shouldn't think they are, now. The money's gone, so they've probably gone too."

"If Landon's here, they may come back. . . . I think we ought to tell the police."

"Then everyone else will get the story. Let's go on a bit first."

"We could easily run into trouble."

"Not if we're careful."

I gave a wry smile. Twice, in the past, I'd made a resolution never to let Mollie lead me into this sort of situation again—yet having got so far it was difficult to turn back. I felt certain *she* wouldn't turn back. It had been her hunch, and she was going to see it through. I said, "Well, we'll go a little way." It sounded pretty weak, but what could I do? At least, I thought, we'd have plenty of light now. I tried on the potholer's helmet, but it had been made for a different-sized head and wasn't comfortable on me. The leather belt with the lamp seemed a better bet. I debated whether to bother with the boiler-suit, and decided not to. I stuck my raincoat in a niche in the rock and fastened the belt round my waist. The light from the lamp was brilliant. I gave Mollie the torch, and stuffed a couple of magnesium flares in my pocket, and we started off along the passage. We had to walk crouched for a few yards, and then the ceiling rose and the passage widened and we were able to move forward side by side in comfort. The floor was dry and the air, though cool, wasn't unpleasantly cold.

We kept going for about fifty yards in a straight line and then stopped to listen. The silence seemed absolute. We went on again, cautiously, and presently we reached a right-angled bend and turned. At once I became aware of a faint sound ahead. At first I couldn't identify it—it was a sort of hoarse murmur, a vibration rather than a sound. Then, as we drew closer, I realised it was water. The murmur increased to a roar. Suddenly we emerged into another chamber. The air was full of a fine mist that soaked our faces. From a rift in the rock high up on our left, a stream of water was pouring in a great cascade and breaking in spray on the floor of the cave. There it formed a stream that flowed away down a steep incline, the left prong of a fork. There was negotiable rock beside the stream, but the way looked very wet. The right prong was higher and drier and looked so much more inviting that we took it automatically. It had a lot of turnings, usually at right-angles, but it didn't divide again and there were no real difficulties. If this was potholing, it was potholing in comfort.

We continued down an easy slope for perhaps ten minutes. We could no longer hear the water. Complete silence had fallen again. I began to wonder where we were going to finish up. Some of these passages, I'd read, ran for miles. . . . Then, abruptly, the sides of the tunnel widened out and the ground fell away in front of us and we jerked to a stop on the edge of darkness. I got down on my knees and groped ahead, and there was nothing but empty space. The powerful beams of my lamp showed nothing at all. I found a fragment of rock and hurled it straight out into the emptiness and when it finally landed the sound was so far away it was barely audible. I picked up another fragment and dropped it over the edge. There was a brief moment of silence and then it hit the bottom. The precipice, if it was that, didn't seem to be a very deep one. I borrowed Mollie's torch and shone it down. The rock edge was almost sheer, but not quite. I could probably have climbed down if there'd been any point. As it was, it seemed better to go back and try the other passage.

It was then that Mollie suddenly said, "I think I can smell paraffin!"

I sniffed. There *was* a curious smell, very faint but very characteristic. I thought she was right—it was paraffin. But I couldn't imagine where it was coming from. There was no sound from below, no light, nothing.

After a moment, curiosity got the better of caution. The alternative to revealing our presence was to retreat in ignorance—and whatever was down there, we couldn't come to any harm on our ledge. I took one of the magnesium flares from my pocket and put a match to it and dropped it into the chasm. The light was blinding, and for a moment we were dazzled and drew back. Then, as our eyes got used to it, we stared in wonder at one of the most awe-inspiring sights I'd ever seen. We were about twenty feet above the floor of a vast cavern, large enough to swallow a house. The roof, even in that brilliant light, was too high to be visible. The cavern itself was a fairy landscape, with weird formations of amber limestone spread around the floor in infinite variety. There was a bunch of stalactite that looked like a frozen waterfall, and a rock cascade furrowed by gigantic flutings. There were things that looked like delicate coral fabrics, and obelisks, and organ pipes, and fantastically tortured sculptings. The spectacle was unbelievably beautiful, and we stood spellbound till the flare burned out.

As darkness fell again, blacker than ever, a voice came echoing up out of the cavern! It seemed to come from somewhere away on the right, and was muffled, as though it had travelled round corners. But the words were clear enough. "*Who's there?*" it said. Eerily, the question was repeated over and over till it died in a whisper.

I cupped my hands and called, slowly and distinctly, "Who are *you?*"

"Landon!" the voice came back. "Arthur Landon. *Help . . .!*"

Mollie said, "God, we've found him . . .!"

I called again. "Are you alone?"

"Yes."

That was all I wanted to know. I cupped my hands for the last time. "Right . . .! I'm coming down to you."

Chapter Thirteen

Mollie's face was tense. She leaned over the edge, examining the rock, and for an anxious moment I thought she was going to say she'd try to climb down too. But even she drew the line at that. "You'll have to go alone,", she said. "I'd never make it. . . . I'll wait for you here."

"Will you be all right?"

"Of course. I'll have the torch. But be careful." I swivelled my belt lamp slightly to one side so that it wouldn't get in the way, and lowered myself cautiously over the edge. Mollie shone her light down the rock face to help me. For a moment or two I hung by my hands, scraping around for a toe-hold. Then I began slowly to descend. I'd done a good deal of rock-climbing in my time, some of it severe, but I'd never been on rock underground before and I didn't at all care for it. Twenty feet wasn't far but it was quite far enough for a disastrous fall, especially when there were sharp spikes of stalagmite all ready to impale me below. The worst danger was that I'd put my weight on something brittle and suddenly lose my main support. Finding reliable holds in the semi-darkness wasn't at all easy. I'd certainly never made a slower descent. But I kept going, and in a few minutes I was safely at the bottom.

I called up to Mollie that I'd made it, and at once set off across the floor of the cavern in the direction the voice had seemed to come from. Near the wall the ground was littered with stalagmite obstructions but as I moved towards the centre the going became better, with nothing worse than rubble and cave-earth to negotiate. Twice I stopped and called "Where are you, Landon?" and an echoing voice came back. I crossed a shallow stream, a mere trickle over the floor. Presently I became aware of a faint glow ahead. Landon must have a light after all. I couldn't understand why I hadn't seen it before. Then, as I drew nearer, I realised that the glow was coming from behind a projecting wall of rock, as the voice had done. I quickened my pace, and reached the jutting rock. As I rounded it, a most astonishing sight met my eyes.

There was a deep alcove—a cave within a cave. Inside it, a complete camp had been set up. There was a small bivouac tent guyed to limestone projections, with rugs spread around it and a camp-chair near the entrance. Behind it there was a great heap of stores—bottles and boxes and cans of every description. In front of the tent there was a paraffin pressure heater, going full blast, and a paraffin lamp with an incandescent mantle that gave an excellent light. There was a man sitting in the chair. I could see he was Landon, though he no longer looked much like his picture. His face, where it wasn't covered by a stubble of beard, was bleached a parchment white. His long thin nose looked sharp as a knife. His eyes were sunk in his head. His hair was in disorder. He was wearing a wind-cheater over a polo-necked sweater, and thick khaki trousers, filthy with damp cave mud. On his feet, incongruously, were a pair of scarlet bedroom slippers.

As I approached he raised himself from the chair and took an uncertain step towards me, swaying a little as though his long imprisonment had weakened him.

"Who *are* you?" he asked in a shaky voice.

I held his arm, steadying him. "I'm a newspaper reporter," I said. "My name's Curtis. I'm the *Record* man who came up with your daughter to bring the money."

Relief flooded his face—relief, and incredulity. He grasped my hand in both his. He was trembling. "How did you find me? How did you know I was here?"

I told him briefly about Mollie, and how we'd followed Clara and seen the ribbed footmarks and suddenly stumbled on the pothole entrance. He shook his head slowly, as though it was all beyond him. I told him about the passage we'd taken, and the ledge I'd climbed down from, and that Mollie was up there now, waiting.

"I can hardly believe it," he said. He looked quite dazed. "It seems like a miracle...."

"Let's hope our luck holds!" I said. "Tell me about the kidnappers—are they coming back?"

"They said they'd be back. They said they'd come at ten o'clock to-night to release me. That was last night, after they'd collected the money. I didn't know whether to believe them or not. I still don't. But I think they may come—to release me or to kill me!"

"What sort of men are they?"

"One of them is young, perhaps thirty, with short, cropped hair. He has a very deep voice. The other is much older, about my age. They're educated men, very sardonic and efficient. I still haven't seen their faces. When they're with me they always wear masks—children's comic masks! Hideous things. They joke about them. One of them wears a steel helmet and a canvas suit when he comes—the other one doesn't bother. The younger one always has a gun—it was he who made me walk out of Clara's house. ..."

Now that he'd started talking he was obviously eager to go on, but I had to interrupt him. There were a hundred things I wanted to know, but the details would have to wait. The first thing was to get out. I looked at my watch. It wasn't quite eight-thirty. If the kidnappers weren't going to be back till ten, we still had some time. I said, "How did *you* get down here?" I knew he hadn't come over the ledge, because he obviously hadn't known of its existence till I'd told him.

"They brought me along a passage with a stream running through it," he said. "The one that starts by the waterfall—the one you didn't take. The passage comes out up there...." He pointed to the wall of rock on his left. "About forty feet up. They've got a folding ladder made of steel wire. That's how I got here. Every time they come, they let it down, and every time they leave they draw it up behind them, so that I'm shut in. They've taken my shoes away, so that I can't try to climb out. They know I was once a good rock-climber—I don't know how."

I shone my lamp on the rock face. It was much smoother, as

well as much higher, than the one I'd come down. I said, "It looks impossible to me, shoes or no shoes."

"I think it is. . . . Even when I was young I don't think I could have done it. But perhaps I could climb up on to your ledge."

"I doubt if you could make that, either," I said. "You've had a bad time—you don't look in good shape for climbing. . . ."

"I'm all right, I assure you. They treated me quite well, you know. They brought all this stuff down for me—they prepared the camp and made it comfortable. I've had warm clothes and plenty of food, tinned food, and light, and water from the stream—even some books to read. Oh, yes, they've looked after me. . . ." His voice cracked. "But I've been here for eight days—alone, except for their short visits. It's a long time to be alone in a cave, eight days! Every day seems like a year. And I wasn't sure I should ever get out again . . . I did all I could . . . I even floated paper boats down the stream that runs across the floor, with messages on them, hoping they'd reach daylight and be read by someone—but of course it didn't work. In the end, I almost lost hope—that's why I'm like this. . . . Despair saps your strength. . . . But I'll be all right now. I'll get to the ledge—you'll see!"

I couldn't have felt more doubtful. His face was wet with sweat, his hands were clasping and unclasping convulsively. He looked a nervous wreck to me. I said, "Well, I don't know . . ." hesitating. I wanted to get him out, but not in pieces. He took a step forward, and stumbled against me. It was all he could do to stand. I knew then that it was impossible.

"No," I said, "it's too great a risk without a rope. . . . Look, suppose I go back to the ledge and out to the waterfall and come back along the other passage—the one you used. I can do it in half an hour. Then I can lower the ladder to you and you can climb up."

He shook his head. "They always take the ladder away with them when they go. They're afraid potholers may come in and find it and climb down. They hide it somewhere—I don't know where. I think it would be better if you fetched help—the police. . . ."

I nodded. In view of his condition, that obviously *was* the best thing to do. If Mollie and I left straight away and raced back to Castleton we could probably have a police party at the pothole well before ten. If the kidnappers returned then, as they'd promised, we'd have a good chance of catching them. If they didn't, we could at least rescue Landon without risk of accident.

"Right," I said, "we'll get the police. . . . If the kidnappers show up before we do you'll have to pretend that nothing's happened—but with luck they won't. We'll do our best, anyway."

"Thank you," he said. "*Thank you!*"

He turned, and sank into the camp-chair, and covered his face with his hands. It was difficult to see in him the confident, brilliant physicist on whom the country had relied a week ago. His ordeal had broken him—he seemed no more than the shadow of a man. I hated leaving him—but I could think of no better way to serve him.

Speed, now, was the most important thing. I left the alcove and set off quickly across the cavern floor. As soon as Mollie saw my light she flashed her own, so that I knew where to make for. In a few moments I was at the foot of the rock. I rested for a short while, steadying myself for the ascent. That was something that couldn't be hurried. Presently I began to climb. It was easier going up, because Mollie's torch lit up the handholds above me. In five minutes I was beside her on the ledge. I explained the situation in a few words, and she didn't argue. In a real crisis, she never argued. We rushed back along the passage at breakneck speed and reached the fork where the stream ran in and continued along the tunnel towards the entrance. The last stretch was wet, where before it had been dry, and as we emerged into the store chamber we realised why. It was raining hard outside. Water was streaming into the swallow and pouring over the floor. We were going to have a wet dash to Castleton. I grabbed my raincoat from the niche where I'd thrust it and was just going to put it on when Mollie caught my arm. "Hugh!" she cried.

I swung round. "What's the matter?"

"The tin hat!" she said. "It's gone!"

Chapter Fourteen

I stared at the heap of stores. It was true—the helmet had gone. So, I now saw, had the boiler-suit. Someone had obviously entered the pothole after we had. I shone my lamp on the ground, and there were footmarks there that had been made since the rain had started. We hadn't noticed them till then because we'd been in such a hurry to leave, but they were plain enough. They were a man's prints—not the ribbed ones we'd picked up on the moor, but smooth ones, with rubber heels. The conclusion seemed inescapable. One of the kidnappers must have returned before time and gone on in by the left-hand fork while we were still in the right one. Presumably he'd come to release Landon—but we couldn't bank on that. There was always the outside chance that he'd come to kill him.

The discovery knocked our plans sideways. If we went for the police now, the rescue party would almost certainly arrive too late to affect the Landon issue, and the kidnapper might well have made his escape. Once he'd gone, there'd be little chance of ever catching him. The alternative was to go in after him. If he was the man with the gun it could be risky—though with three of us around he might well hesitate to shoot. If he wasn't, I thought I could probably handle him. I put it to Mollie, and she said at once, "Let's go back." We turned, and began to retrace our steps.

The noise as we approached the waterfall was louder than it had been. The flow from the cleft had increased as a result of the rain and the roar in the chamber was deafening. We got very wet skirting the cascade, and I could well understand why our kidnapper had equipped himself with a boiler-suit. What I couldn't understand was why the other one hadn't. But we were much too excited now to bother about trifles like that. With a desperate man trapped in front of us, we'd got to watch our step all the way. I warned Mollie to be ready to switch her light off the moment we saw or heard anything, and went cautiously ahead.

The passage was very different from the first one we'd taken. That had seemed dead—probably it had been abandoned by the waters thousands of years ago. This one, with a stream running through it, was alive and spectacular. The water had built up its own clay and pebble dams, so that there was a chain of wide, still pools that reflected and doubled the exquisite beauties of the rock. Our lights kept picking out lovely sheets of crystalline enamel, and silken curtains petrified as though by a spell, and delicate limestone flowers in rock niches. But we had little eye for beauty now—the going was treacherous, with slabs of soft, slippery clay lying between young growths of stalagmite that snapped and crackled beneath our feet.

After about twenty yards the passage divided. To the left there was an upward-going tunnel that looked as though it might well lead to another exit. Wherever it went to, it wasn't the one for us—the rubber heel marks continued on beside the stream. We kept going. Presently the passage took a sharp dip and for a few yards the water raced downhill beside us in a series of miniature cataracts. As we descended, the roof got lower, forcing us to crouch and finally to crawl. It was knee marks in the clay that we were following now—and other, older marks, made I imagined by the boxes of stores that must have been hauled along there.

Suddenly, as we stopped for a moment to rest, I thought I caught a sound above the murmur of the water. I called softly to Mollie to douse her light and switched mine off too. I looked ahead—and knew that I hadn't been mistaken. There was a bend in the passage just in front of us, and from round the corner came a glow of light. Someone was coming towards us with a lamp! There was something very peculiar about his movements, too. It sounded as though he was dragging himself along on his stomach—yet there was certainly no need for that. With over three feet of headroom, it was an easy crawl. A chill ran through me. He *could* be dragging someone else along!

I inched forward in the darkness and took up a position just before the bend, keeping away from the stream and close to the inside wall so that I'd have the greatest possible cover. I unhooked the lamp from my belt and put it on the floor three feet away to my left, still switched off but pointing forwards. If the kidnappers had a gun and started shooting when the lights went up, I'd be happier not to be in line with the lamp. I whispered to Mollie to come up close behind me. I didn't quite know what I was going to do, but we were committed now to the encounter—and at least we should have the advantage of surprise. . . . The shuffling noise grew louder. I peered round the corner of the rock. The light was much nearer, but its direct beam was obscured by something. By whatever was making the shuffling noise, I thought. It was all horribly eerie.

I daren't let the man come too close. Once he was round the bend we'd be sitting targets. I waited till I thought he was near enough for the beam of my lamp to reach him. Then I stretched my hand out, and pressed the switch, and drew back quickly into the shelter of the wall.

There was a sharp gasp ahead. Very cautiously, I peered out again. For a moment, all I could see was the outline of a suitcase! It was the friction of the case, being pushed along the floor, that had made the shuffling noise. Then a brilliant light appeared beside it—the light from a helmeted head. I couldn't see the man's face, because the beam was shining straight at me, dazzling me. For a second or two there was no sound. Then a sharp voice said, "Who's that?"

I could hardly believe my ears—but I knew that voice. It was the voice of Ronald Barr!

Chapter Fifteen

I was so staggered that for a moment I couldn't get a word out. Barr was the very last man I'd have expected to meet down there. Particularly with the suitcase! It was, without any doubt, the one Clara and I had brought the money in—and judging by the difficulty he'd had in pushing it along, it was still full. The wildest suspicions began to race through my mind.

"Who is it?" Barr repeated in a harsher tone.

I said, "It's Hugh Curtis—and Mollie Bourne of the *Courier*."

A sigh escaped him—a long sigh of relief. "God, you scared me. ... I thought you were one of the kidnappers."

I swivelled my lamp so that it shone on the passage wall and not straight at him. "Take your helmet off," I said, "your light's blinding me." He took it off and put it down on the floor so that his lamp also shone on the wall. Now we could both see each other. He was wearing the boiler-suit, and it was thick with cave mud. He looked filthy.

I said, "What the devil are *you* doing here?"

"That's a long story. Trying to find Arthur Landon, as a matter of fact. ... I suppose you followed us in?"

"Us?"

"Of course. ..." He turned and called back along the passage, "Come on, Clara—your newspaper pals are here."

So she was there too! Mollie murmured in my ear, "You see!" I didn't see at all. The whole situation was completely beyond me. We waited. Presently there was a scrambling sound behind Barr, and Clara appeared. She stared at us, but didn't speak. Her face was as white as chalk.

I said, "I still don't understand.... How did you get on to this place?"

"We'll tell you later, Curtis—there's no time now."

"What are you doing with that suitcase?"

"We found it along the passage.... Look, we're pretty sure Landon's here somewhere but we need help—we're actually on our way now to get the police.... The explanations'll have to wait."

It was on the tip of my tongue to tell him we knew where Landon was—but I didn't. I didn't trust him, and I didn't want to tell him anything—I wanted to listen. I no longer had any feeling of urgency. By my watch the time was twenty minutes to ten, so we'd missed our chance to fetch help. If we tried to leave now we might easily run slap into the kidnappers. If we stayed where we were, and they came, we could retreat into the pothole and probably find some way of coping with them.

I said, "I think we'd like to hear your story first."

At that, Clara found her voice. "Hugh, it'll take ages.... I'm sure Father must be here, and if he is the main thing's to get him out.... All we need is a big party to search...."

"Look," I said, "you were supposed to be waiting at the hotel for your father's return. Instead of that you sneaked up here to the pothole, which you obviously knew about. How did you know about it? Barr was supposed to be in London. Instead of that, he's here with you. Why? I think I'm entitled to an explanation—and I mean to have one. What's going on?"

There was a moment's silence. Then Clara said, "I suppose you'd better tell them, Ronald—but do hurry...."

Barr shrugged. "All right—I'll keep it short.... You'll probably be damned annoyed, Curtis, but it's nothing to do with Clara, it was entirely my doing.... The thing is, I never really reconciled myself to letting you and Clara bring the money to the kidnappers on your own. I was still worried about what might happen to Clara, and I wanted to be around. So when she left home yesterday morning I followed her in my car, and saw you pick her up at Marble Arch—and then I followed you."

I stared at him. "You mean—all the way?"

"All the way."

"I didn't see you."

"You weren't meant to. . . . Anyway, you were too busy keeping your eye on Miss Bourne's car to be interested in me. I was behind her."

"*I* didn't see you, either," Mollie said.

"Of course you didn't—all you were bothering about was Curtis. Anyhow, that's what happened. I followed you, and I saw you both stop on the road, and I saw you again in that village. I parked behind a lorry there—I wasn't more than thirty yards away. I could even see you arguing! After that I shadowed you all the way to Mam Tor. When you stopped there and got out I shoved my car behind some rocks and climbed the hillside opposite and watched you inspecting the foot of the precipice through your glasses. I realised you must be reconnoitring the meeting place, but I couldn't believe the kidnappers really intended meeting you at the foot—the place looked much too enclosed. Then I suddenly had the idea they might try and haul the money up from the top. . . ."

"You thought of that!" Mollie said. "You *were* bright."

"I wouldn't call it particularly bright—it seemed obvious. . . . Anyhow, at dusk I walked round to the top of the precipice and waited there, flat on my face in a little hollow. And sure enough, at eight o'clock two men arrived. It was very dark, and though they had a torch they hardly used it, so I couldn't see much. But I could hear their voices and I could tell by the sounds that they were lowering a rope and then hauling something up. The whole thing only took a few minutes. . . . Well, having got that far I couldn't let them just disappear, so I followed *them*. I followed them right to the entrance to this pothole. I still couldn't see much, but it was pretty clear they were going down into some sort of hole. I didn't dare follow them in, and I didn't want to leave the place in the dark in case I couldn't find it again. So I stuck around all night, and damned cold it was! I'd taken the precaution of putting some food in my pocket or I'd never have lasted. Anyway, in the morning they both came out. I'd had to take cover rather far away so I couldn't see them too well, but this time I did manage to get a glimpse of them. . . ."

"What were they like?" By now I was fascinated. I wouldn't have called it a brief narrative, but it was certainly gripping.

"One was youngish, stocky, with a sort of crew cut. The other was a good deal older—quite grey, in fact. He seemed to be taking the lead. They both had fawn raincoats on. They walked away over the moors, talking hard. The younger one had a very low-pitched voice. . . . As soon as they were clear away, I went down the hole to have a look round. By now I thought it quite likely Landon was here—it was obviously the kidnappers' base, and it was a jolly good hiding place. I found this boiler-suit and helmet just inside the entrance, so I borrowed them. Even with the helmet lamp, though, I damn nearly got lost. I tried a passage that forked away to the right but it suddenly ended at a big cave with a vertical drop and that was that. Then I came along this one a little way and almost got stuck in a tunnel that strikes up to the left—you probably saw it. I didn't like it at all, I can tell you—not on my own. So I went back to the entrance—it was late afternoon by then—and left the suit and helmet there and walked down to the road to telephone Clara and come clean about what I'd been up to and see what she thought about raising a search party. . . ."

"You telephoned Clara!" I broke in.

"I did."

"How did you know where she was staying?"

"I'd heard one of the men on Mam Tor say to the other, 'They're going to the George at Castleton.' Don't ask me how *they* knew. Anyway, I found a phone box and rang Clara, and by luck she was in, and I told her everything that had happened and said I thought there was a good chance her father was in the pothole. She was absolutely furious at first. She said her father was going to be released that evening anyway and that by interfering I was probably endangering his life. She said I shouldn't have come up, shouldn't have followed the kidnappers, shouldn't have done anything. She was livid. I thought she was being crazy. I said she'd no guarantee whatever that the kidnappers wouldn't come back to the pothole and kill Landon and that if he was there we ought to get him out while the going was good. She said perhaps he wasn't there—perhaps it was just a cache for the money. She was terribly nervous about doing anything. But in the end she agreed to come up to the moor and discuss things. I told her the way, and she came, and we met...."

"That couldn't have been easy," Mollie said, "in the dark."

"It wasn't—I wished afterwards I'd arranged to meet her on the road, but I was anxious not to be away from the pothole any longer than I could help in case the kidnappers slipped back in without my knowing.... We more or less stumbled across each other in the end. We'd no idea you two were around, of course. We sat on a rock and had another long talk. Clara was still against the search party idea, because it couldn't possibly be arranged quietly. I said in that case why didn't we take another look in the hole ourselves? By now it had started to pour with rain and she had to make a decision one way or the other. Finally she said okay, and we came in and took this passage again because I hadn't fully explored it. Actually, there are several more forks—it'll take quite a while to explore them all. We followed this stream for about half a mile but we didn't see any sign of Landon. What we did find was the suitcase with the money in it—it was on a ledge, at a kind of dead end where the stream ducks under a rock. We had another discussion there. I said that, assuming Landon was in the pothole, it was obvious the kidnappers *weren't* going to keep their promise to release him by ten, because time was getting on and they'd have been back by now. I said it was more likely they were going to let him die here, and come back and collect the money later when the heat was off it. That finally persuaded Clara. She said, all right, perhaps we'd better go to the police after all and get a proper search party mobilised.... And that's exactly what we're doing."

"With the money!" I said.

"Well, naturally.... We didn't want the kidnappers to come back in our absence and clear off with it. My idea about them leaving it for a while was only a guess."

I nodded slowly. I didn't know what to make of him. He was either very genuine, or very glib. His story rang true up to a point—yet there were things about it that somehow didn't fit. . . . The whole pattern of behaviour seemed odd. . . .

Suddenly I thought of something. "Back at the entrance," I said, "we saw your footmarks on the wet ground. We didn't see Clara's. How was that?"

"Good God, man," he broke out, "what are you so suspicious about . . .? I gave her a hump on my back over the worst bits, that's all. . . . Now I suggest we stop wasting time. Some of us can fetch help, and the others can stick around in case the kidnappers come back. . . . Let's get out of here."

"Yes, *please* let's go," Clara said. "I'm sorry we did it all on our own, Hugh—I suppose I ought to have told you, but everything happened so quickly"

I said, "Have we had the true story, Clara? You've been very quiet."

"Of course you have," she said. "The whole truth and nothing but the truth. . . . Why ever not?"

It was then that Mollie suddenly cried, "Hugh!—look at the stream!"

I looked—and promptly forgot everything else. When we'd stopped, it had been flowing gently between its clay dams, making scarcely a murmur. Now it was a vigorous current, and the tops of the dams were covered. Even as I watched, it lapped right across the passage floor. The level was rising fast.

It didn't need a genius to know what was happening. The rain outside had obviously got worse. The storm waters from above were pouring down into the tunnel—and we were in one of the lowest sections of it!

Chapter Sixteen

There was a moment or two of confusion. Mollie started to move towards the exit. Barr had clapped his helmet on his head and was pushing the suitcase towards me. But Clara, instead of following him, had turned and begun to go back the way she'd come. Barr stopped and shouted to her, "This way, you idiot!" She shouted something in reply. It sounded like "*Father* . . .!" Barr left the case and went after her. I called to Mollie to wait and went after Barr. If Clara was worrying about Landon, the only thing was to tell her we knew where he was and that he'd be safe enough in his vast cavern however much water came in. But I didn't have to—by the time I reached them Barr had calmed her, and we all scrambled back together. I said, "Okay, Mollie, step on it!" and we set off again towards the exit. Barr was still pushing the suitcase ahead of him.

We ran into trouble almost at once. The water wasn't deep yet but the current was strong enough to make every movement an effort. Now that the Moor was completely covered there was no way of avoiding the treacherous clay patches, and our knees slid wildly over them. The ground was uneven, and we kept plunging into invisible holes. Barr soon had to abandon the case. Then Clara was thrown off balance and lost her torch. We waited while she caught up. The water surged round our thighs as we knelt. The current was much fiercer now. We'd begun to climb, and it was rushing down at us with real weight behind it.

Conditions grew steadily worse. At the very steep bit, the stream was a roaring torrent. The scene under the low roof was indescribably awful. The din was deafening. For a minute or two we battled on, clutching at the rock wall for support—but now I'd begun to doubt if we'd make it. Uphill, we were sliding helplessly on the clay and losing as much ground as we were gaining. The weight of water was too great for us—we were only exhausting ourselves to no purpose. A wave washed over my lamp and it went out. I cried, "Mollie!—we must go back!" I grabbed her arm, and we turned. "Back!" I shouted to Barr, above the roaring water. "We must go with the stream!" He nodded. He was clinging to a lump of stalagmite, and holding Clara. She looked terrified. We went past them, and they turned behind us.

Now, by comparison, the going was easy. The fast-flowing stream swept us along. In places we were almost floating. Mollie was a little ahead of me. She'd given me her torch and I was trying to hold it above the water. Barr's head lamp was still working. We passed the submerged suitcase. The roof began to lift a little. We were carried round a bend that was new to me. . . .

Quite suddenly, the passage seemed to grow quiet. There was turbulence in the water, but no longer any current. The stream was getting a lot deeper, very quickly. I could see it lapping up the wall inches at a time. I couldn't understand it. . . . Then, with a pang of real fear, I knew! Barr had spoken of the stream ducking under a rock. But not all this water—not through a tiny opening. It was flooding back! The whole passage was going to fill up like a bath!

We struggled on—there was nothing else to do. We were swimming now. The water was bitterly cold, and I knew we couldn't last long. Suddenly Clara gave a panic-stricken scream. I looked back. Barr was helping her. He'd have to manage—I couldn't leave Mollie. She was flagging, too. I drew alongside her and urged her on. She was a wonderful swimmer but her clothes were hampering her. She hadn't had time to get out of her raincoat and no one could have swum far in that. The roof was only a foot above the water now. We were going to be trapped like rats. Suddenly she went down. I put a hand under her and raised her up, gasping and choking. With my other hand I was still holding the torch. I kicked out with my legs as hard as I could. The last effort . . .! At that moment the torch beam lit up a break in the tunnel wall. There was a fork, and the passage on the right rose steeply, well above water level. I shouted, "Keep going—we'll make it!" I could sense the light of Barr's lamp behind me. Clara had stopped screaming. We were going to get through after all. I reached the fork and struggled out on to the clayey bank and heaved Mollie up beside me.

Barr was about ten yards behind, holding Clara. Suddenly he shouted, "Curtis!—help!" I gave the torch to Mollie and went back in and struck out for the head lamp. There was a choking cry from Clara. She had panicked again, and was struggling. Before I could reach them the head lamp went under, and out. Barr cried in a desperate tone, "Curtis!—I've lost her!" I swam towards the voice, but in the darkness I couldn't find him. He was splashing wildly around, searching for Clara. There was no sound from her. I swam to and fro across the passage, groping about for the touch of a dress. But there was nothing. Presently I swam back to the pinpoint of light that was Mollie's torch. Barr, exhausted by his frantic efforts, was climbing out. Mollie, her face drawn with horror, was shining the torch down. The dark water was lapping at the tunnel roof. I climbed out, too, and looked down. For a second I thought I saw something disappearing into the tunnel—something white. It could have been a drowned face. In a moment it had gone. There was nothing now but a few bubbles.

Chapter Seventeen

For a moment we stood there as though paralysed. It didn't seem possible that Clara was dead. The fact that the rest of us had barely escaped the same fate didn't make it any more credible. We *had* escaped—why couldn't she have done? The suddenness, the finality, was numbing. The horror of it all was heightened by our ghastly surroundings. Mollie said, "Oh, God!" and leaned back against the wall, her head in her hands. Barr didn't move—he just gazed unbelievingly down at the water. I felt I had to say something to him, though it was hard to find words. The tragedy must be so appalling for him that anything I said could only sound empty. . . . Then he turned to look at me. His face registered many emotions—shock, uncertainty, even fear—but no one would have guessed that the girl he loved had just drowned before his eyes. If this was grief, I didn't recognise it.

I was right not to. As I started to say something, he snapped, "Spare me your sympathy—she meant nothing to me!"

I stared at him. "Meant nothing . . .! But you were going to marry her."

"That slut! Never!"

The callous words, the savage tone, drove all gentler emotions from the tunnel like a wind dispersing fog. Mollie looked up sharply. Barr's expression was contemptuous. He seemed like a man who'd suddenly decided to throw off a mask he no longer needed. I began to readjust my own ideas. I remembered what Mollie had said about Clara's "revulsion" when Barr had kissed her. At last I had no difficulty in believing that. Now it appeared that the revulsion had been mutual. That added up to only one thing—the relationship they'd paraded before the world had been merely one of convenience. They'd disliked each other, yet they'd needed each other, right up to those last few moments when Barr had made such desperate efforts to save her. What had been between them?

I was bursting with questions, but this was no time to ask them. We'd been badly shocked, and we were soaked to the skin. The passage was icy, and we were shivering with cold. Unless we got moving again there'd be no future for any of us. I shone the torch around. For the moment, there was only one way to go. The tunnel we'd come through was blocked, and it would probably be many hours before we could return that way to the entrance. The water at our feet was still rising, though slowly. I said, "Come on, Mollie, let's see where this passage leads."

As we turned, Barr said, "I can tell you where it leads."

"Oh! Where?"

"It comes out above the cave where Landon is."

I stopped short. "Then you *did* find him . . .!"

He made a derisive sound. "Of course we found him. As we already knew where he was, there wasn't much difficulty! When we met you, we'd just talked to him. We knew *you'd* talked to him. We knew everything."

The mask was right down now! Or was it? Cold or not, I couldn't leave things there. I said, "Why all that pretence in the tunnel, then?"

"There were good reasons for that, but it'll take time to tell you."

"If you knew Landon was here, why didn't you try to get him out? Why leave him for the kidnappers?"

For a moment Barr regarded me sardonically. Then he said, "My dear fellow, there never were any kidnappers!"

"No *kidnappers* . . .!"

"A pure invention . . . Landon wasn't kidnapped. He faked everything to look as though he had been, that's all. The ransom letters were all written by him. The telephone calls from the supposed kidnappers were faked on his instructions. He organised everything.

Far from being kidnapped, he hid himself away here of his own accord."

It seemed incredible. "Why would he do that . . .?"

"Because he wanted the ransom money, of course."

"You mean he faked the whole thing for personal gain?"

"That's exactly it. Landon's a genius gone wrong. Now you know the truth."

I very much doubted that! "And what are you?" I asked. "Where do you come into it?"

"I'm entirely on the level, though I realise it may not seem so to you at the moment."

"I'll say it doesn't. What were you and Clara doing here? What have you been up to?"

"I can explain everything, Curtis, but it's pretty involved. . . . Look, why don't we go down and join Landon, and I'll tell you the whole story while we get warm. We'll only freeze to death if we stay talking here."

That made sense, if nothing else did. I took Mollie's arm and helped her up the short, steep slope that led away from the stream. There was a bend, and almost at once we were looking down into the great cavern. At the point where we'd emerged from the stream, we'd only been a few yards away from it. Landon's encampment lay a little to the left of us, forty feet below. The paraffin fire and lamp were burning brightly and looked most inviting. I couldn't see any sign of Landon. I shone the torch down on the ground. Near the edge of the rock, two iron pitons had been driven into cracks. One end of a rolled-up steel wire ladder was attached to them. Beside the ladder there was a coil of nylon rope, also made fast.

I stood well back with Mollie while Barr unrolled the ladder and lowered it over the edge. I trusted him less than ever. It was true he'd suddenly become very forthcoming about a lot of things, but with the tunnel closed behind him and Landon's cavern so near, a certain amount of frankness had been more or less forced on him. He must have realised that we'd go up the slope and find the cavern ourselves, and once we'd found it we'd obviously go down and talk to Landon again. Whatever there was to be discovered, we'd have discovered it in the end. All Barr had done so far was to go along with the inevitable. He'd need watching all the time.

As the ladder touched bottom, he stepped back. "All ready, Miss Bourne. There's nothing to worry about—we'll tie the rope to you and use it as a safety line." He had the end of the rope in his hand.

"*I'll* do it," I said. "And I'd feel much happier if you kept out of the way. Here, take the torch."

He shrugged. "You've got me all wrong, Curtis, but I suppose I'd better humour you." He withdrew a little way up the passage, and sat down.

I said, "All right, Mollie?"

She nodded.

I made the rope fast round her. She was shaking with cold and looked exhausted, but she was very game. She knelt down with her back to the cavern and gripped the top of the ladder and got her feet into the rungs. Then, slowly, she began to descend. I took a turn with the rope round a rock projection and held it with only a little slack, ready to take the strain if she slipped. I didn't think she would—in this sort of situation she could usually call up reserves of nerve and strength. I was more concerned about Barr. I kept one eye on him all the time. The ladder had begun to sway unpleasantly with no one at the bottom to hold it, but Mollie was nearly down. If I had to, I could safely let go of the rope now. Barr had made no move. It was all right. I felt the rope swing free as Mollie reached the ground and untied it. She waved, and I hauled it up.

Barr got to his feet. "Okay, Curtis—you go ahead."

"After you," I said, and moved away from the edge.

"My God, you're suspicious."

"With thirty thousand pounds back there in the tunnel," I said, "I'd be a fool not to be."

"It's under water—you know that."

"It won't be for ever. If anything happened to me, you could have another crack at getting it out, couldn't you?"

119

"I told you—I was taking it to the police."

"You told me a lot of things. Most of them weren't true."

For a moment he looked very nasty. I thought he was going to start a rough house there and then, and I braced myself. It would have been a bad place. Perhaps he thought the same thing—or perhaps I was just misjudging him. Anyhow, he didn't do anything.

"Have it your own way," he said. He got on the ladder and went down fast. He was obviously used to it. I followed him as he stepped off. Mollie was standing at the bottom, waiting. At once we started to cross the few yards of uneven floor to the camp. The murmur of the cavern stream was a good deal louder than it had been, but in this great open space it held no menace.

As we moved into the circle of light, Landon suddenly appeared. He'd been in his tent, with the paraffin fire roaring at the entrance, and he evidently hadn't heard us. When he saw us, he stopped short, staring. He was staring mostly at Barr. He seemed to be taking in our sodden clothes, our bedraggled appearance.

"What's happened?" he said—and then, in a sharper tone: "Where's Clara?"

Barr said, "I'm afraid I've got bad news for you, Landon."

"We were trapped by storm water in the tunnel. . . . I don't need to tell you I did my best to help her—but she struggled. . . . She was drowned."

There was a little silence. Landon was as still as the clump of stalagmite behind him.

"Are you quite sure she's dead?" This time he seemed to be speaking to me.

"I'm afraid there's no doubt about it," I said.

"The tunnel's full—right to the roof. . . . I'm sorry."

He still didn't move. His expression was unfathomable. If he was hard hit, he scarcely showed it. No one seemed to be reacting normally to Clara's death. Perhaps *he* hadn't cared about her, either. It wouldn't be surprising. If he'd really behaved in the fantastically criminal way that Barr had said, he must be a very queer bird.

All the same, there was something I felt I must tell him. I said, "When the stream started to rise, Landon, Clara thought of you.

She was worried about you—she must have thought the water would come in here, too. She called out, 'Father ...!' and she started to come back this way on her own. She thought of you and she wanted to be with you. I don't know if it means anything to you—but there it is."

His face softened a little. "Yes—that does mean something to me.... Thank you." He turned his head away. "Poor Clara!" he said.

I still couldn't understand him. His tone was the strangest blend of compassion and dismissal.

I looked round for Barr. He'd already gone off to change into dry clothes. I saw him peering into Landon's tent. Then he started to rummage among the pile of stores beside it. Landon sat down on the rug before the fire. His face, glowing in the orange light, had an extraordinary look of peace. I said, "We'd better find something to change into ourselves, Mollie," and we joined Barr. He had shed his boiler-suit, and was transferring the contents of the pockets to a dark jacket and trousers. After a moment he went off into the shadows. I heard him pouring water for a drink. He obviously knew his way around the cavern as well as Landon himself.

There was no shortage of spare clothes, and after we'd dried off on some towels that Mollie found among the kitchen things behind the tent, we re-equipped ourselves. Mollie fitted herself out with a pair of turned-up slacks and a heavy sweater, and I found a jersey and some curduroys. Then we joined Landon by the fire. The warmth in the alcove was wonderfully restoring. Landon made room for us, but he didn't speak. He seemed to be completely lost in his thoughts. After a moment Barr reappeared and sat down on the other side of Landon.

We made an extraordinary quartette. Landon looked like some wild hermit philosopher. Barr, at the far end of the rug, seemed remote and vaguely menacing. All of us had the appearance of survivors from some frightful cataclysm. The shadow of Clara's death hung over the place. Everything seemed utterly bizarre and unreal. Suddenly Barr began to talk to Landon in a tense and urgent tone. This time there was no pretence at all. He spoke as though Mollie and I weren't there.

"I know just what's in your mind, Landon," he said. "You're thinking that things have changed between us, aren't you, now that Clara's dead? You're thinking that I've no hold over you any longer, that you're free. You're right, of course, in a sense. You're probably thinking that I'm stuck here now till the tunnel clears, and that then you'll hand me over to the police, and that there's nothing I can do about it. You're probably right about that, too. I saw it all coming, the moment Clara died. I dare say you're mentally totting up what I'll get when I'm caught—and I don't blame you. You've every reason to hate me, and it must be a satisfying exercise. I'll get quite a stretch, especially if the sentences run consecutively. . . . Seven years for blackmail, I suppose—five more for conspiracy—not to mention perjury and theft. . . . That's what you're thinking, isn't it?"

Landon said nothing.

"All the same, there's another side to that picture, you know." Barr's voice had taken on a rougher edge.

"You're not exactly in the clear yourself. They'll get *you* for conspiracy and theft, as well as me. And what a conspiracy! What a theft! You'll get a pretty long stretch yourself. And that's not all. You'll be disgraced. You'll be hounded by everyone. You'll be finished, Landon. Your life will be over. Especially as everyone will know the truth about your dear daughter. You're not going to enjoy that very much, are you? You'd be better dead, like Clara."

Landon stirred a little, but still he didn't speak.

"Of course," Barr went on, "you could avoid all that if you wanted to. You could get clean away with everything. You realise that, don't you . . .?" It seemed to me that his harsh tone held a hint of desperation now. "The whole country believes you were kidnapped. You could still pretend that you were. We could hide Clara's body so that it wouldn't be found. She'd simply have disappeared. We could tidy this place up so that everything looked genuine, the way we intended to. It's your only hope, Landon. Yours *and* mine. Our interests are the same. Why rot in jail when we don't have to? I could have the money—you could still have your work and your freedom. . . . Are you with me, Landon? Do you see what I'm driving at? All I need is co-operation. . . . Nobody knows anything about us except these two busybodies—and they've been delivered into our hands. The girl won't give any trouble. I'll do the dirty work. Between us, we can easily deal with Curtis. It's the only way."

I'd already started up. So had Barr. I saw something glinting in his hand. It was a short, murderous-looking knife. I guessed he'd got it from Landon's stores. The sight of it stopped me dead. Barr was holding it defensively and he made no move towards me. "Better sit down, Curtis," he said. "You don't want to argue with this before you have to."

I sank back on the rug, watching him. He subsided, too. Evidently he wasn't sure enough of Landon to launch an attack. Mollie moved a little closer to me. I waited for Landon to speak. I felt far from confident. The man *was* a criminal—that was absolutely clear now. Everything *was* at stake for him. And this cavern would hide all secrets. If the two of them fell on me together, I wouldn't have a chance. I stretched a hand out into the shadows, trying to find a piece of loose rock, but there wasn't anything.

Landon looked at Barr. Then he looked at me. His cheekbones were sharp in the light. His face was as pitiless as an executioner's. The seconds dragged like hours.

Suddenly the tension broke. "You must be out of your mind, Barr," he said. "I've only one aim now—to see you punished. You can put that knife down—it won't help you. If you give the slightest trouble, Curtis and I will join forces against you at once. Is that agreed, Curtis?"

"It'll be a pleasure!" I said. Beside me, Mollie gave a little sigh.

Barr said, "You're a fool, Landon, a stupid fool. You'll live to regret this." His tone was venomous. He'd missed all his chances, and he knew it. I felt sure, now, that he'd intended murder ever since Clara's death. He *had* hoped to catch me off guard on the ledge. His outburst of frankness had been intended merely to disarm me. When that plan had failed he'd been driven back on this last desperate gamble. Now he'd used all his chips. . . . At least, I hoped he had. The morose silence into which he'd fallen certainly suggested it.

One thing was quite clear—we weren't going to get any more information out of him. I turned to Landon.

"Look," I said, "if we're going to be allies, even temporarily, wouldn't it be as well if you told us just what's been happening?"

He ran a hand wearily over his face. "It's a long story, Curtis."

"We're going to be here a long time," I said.

"Well. . ." He hesitated. "You must have picked up a good deal from what's already been said."

"No more than an outline. . . . I gather you faked your own kidnapping for the sake of the ransom money, and that Barr and your daughter were involved in the plot. . . Is that right?"

"Yes, that's right. . . . But I didn't want the money for myself. I had to get it for Barr."

"Because of this hold he had over you?"

"Yes."

"What was his hold?"

There was a little pause. Then Landon said, "My daughter killed a man, and Barr knew about it. . . . She killed a man named Frank Angel."

Chapter Eighteen

I said incredulously, "*Clara* killed him?" I'd been prepared for more surprises, but this was staggering. Not even Lawson had thought of that!

Landon said, "Yes—she shot him."

"Then all that evidence at the inquest . . .?"

"It was all untrue. Clara was visiting Angel, not Barr. After the shooting Barr fixed up her story for her. . . . Until that evening she'd never met him."

It was fascinating. I said, "Landon, I do realise it must be hard for you to talk about it, particularly just now, but it's all got to come out and we know so much already. . . . Won't you tell us from the beginning?"

He was silent for a moment. Then he gave a faint shrug. "I don't mind telling you—in a way I think I'll be glad to get it off my chest. . . ." He paused, as though collecting his thoughts. Then he said: "Angel was a man Clara had met at a party. She had an affair with him. He was completely worthless, like most of the men she knew, but he was very good looking and she was besotted with him. She wanted to marry him, and he'd promised they would marry. Then she discovered that he was being kept by an older woman and was perfectly content to go on being kept and hadn't any intention of marrying her at all. She was furious. She wrote him an angry letter, and the next evening she went round to have it out with him. She'd had quite a lot to drink beforehand, which may have had something to do with what happened. . . . She took a revolver with her. I didn't know she had a revolver, but apparently it had been given her by some army man who'd taken her out to practise shooting. . . . She told me afterwards that she took the gun merely to frighten Angel. I don't know about that. Anyhow, there was a frightful quarrel and—according to Clara—a struggle, and the gun went off."

"It went off twice!" Barr put in. He seemed to have recovered his composure, and was following the story with malicious satisfaction.

"It went off twice," Landon agreed. "Angel fell dead. When Clara saw what she'd done she apparently became panic-stricken. She dropped the gun and rushed out of the flat into the mews. . . . There she almost collided with Barr, who lived in the flat next door. He'd heard the shots and he'd come down to investigate. . . ."

Landon broke off, but only for a moment. Now that he'd started, he was clearly finding it a relief to talk. Presently he went on:

"Barr stopped her and asked her what had happened. She was barely articulate. The door of Angel's flat was still open, and he made her go back there with him. No one else seemed to be bothering about the shots—the occupants of the other two flats in the mews were apparently out for the evening. . . . Barr questioned Clara closely. Among other things he asked her who her parents were, and she told him about me, and where I worked. Barr was a professional blackmailer, and he saw possibilities in the situation. He said he was sure the shooting had been accidental, and that he might be able to help her. He wrapped the gun up carefully and put it in his pocket. He asked Clara if there was anything in the flat connecting her with Angel. There was only one thing she knew about—the letter she'd sent him the day before. Barr found that on the body and pocketed it. Otherwise there seemed to be nothing to suggest she'd known the man. . . ."

Mollie said, "Surely Clara had visited Angel before? Someone might have seen her."

"No, Miss Bourne—Angel had always visited *her*, very discreetly, using the back way into her house, because he'd been afraid his patroness might stop subsidising him if she found out what was happening—so there was no great risk from that point of view. What did worry Clara was the thought that there might be some

126

small thing, like a telephone number written down somewhere, that she didn't know about. Barr said there was only one safe way to take care of that possibility—through *him*. Clara, he said, must pretend she was his fiancée, and that she'd been visiting *him*—and he'd undertake to account for any evidence that might emerge of contact between Clara and Angel, simply by saying that all three of them had been acquainted. Clara needn't worry about anything, he said—he'd do all the talking when the police came. He was very confident and resourceful—he even produced an engagement ring for her, that some girl had returned to him . . .!"

I glanced at Barr. There was the shadow of a grin on his face. Considering how dim his prospects were he was remarkably cheerful again. I didn't much like it—I'd felt easier about him when he was morose.

"Then Barr called the police," Landon went on. "When they came he told his story about hearing shots next door and going down and seeing a woman rushing from the mews. Clara merely had to behave like his fiancée and corroborate what he said. Nobody suspected them of being anything but *bona fide* witnesses in the case. In due course they repeated their story at the inquest. Barr's evidence of various women going to Angel's flat—which actually wasn't true—fitted very well into the picture the police had formed of Angel. The field of suspicion was wide—though in fact it was Angel's patroness, Mrs. Albury, who received most of their attention. . . ."

"Dear Mrs. Albury!" Barr murmured.

Landon continued. "Barr waited till the inquest was over and it was clear that he and Clara had got away with their story. Then he showed his hand. He'd kept the gun, which had Clara's fingerprints on it, and also the letter. He began to talk about money. Clara told him she hadn't got any money, but he said that didn't matter—he'd like to meet me, because he had an idea I might be able to get hold of some. Clara wasn't in a position to refuse his request. She wrote to me and asked me if I would go and see her. I was surprised, because she'd been steadily drifting away from me and lately had avoided seeing me altogether—but I was also very pleased. I went along, and she told me everything. . . . You can imagine how I felt. I was appalled. . . ."

He broke off again. His forehead was suddenly glistening in the firelight. He took out a handkerchief and gently dabbed his face. Then he went on:

"The next evening, Barr came round. Until then, he'd been thinking in terms of a comparatively small amount of money—a few thousands—but now he'd suddenly become much more ambitious because he'd seen the security police car outside Clara's house and concluded that I must occupy a position of exceptional importance at Crede. He was very cool and self-assured and said at once that he expected to be paid handsomely for his silence. I pointed out that he'd already committed perjury at the inquest and therefore wasn't in a position to tell the police anything, but he said he'd been planning to go abroad for some time and that if I didn't pay up he'd post the gun and the letter to the police with a covering note just before he left. I asked him how much he wanted and he said the exact figure would be a matter for discussion and negotiation but the kind of figure he had in mind was of the order of £50,000. I said he was mad—I just didn't have that sort of money and couldn't possibly get hold of it. He said that what I had was knowledge—top secret knowledge that must be worth a fortune in the right quarters—and that I'd better start making plans for selling it. I told him I'd never do that. He said I'd better think it over, because if I didn't find some way of raising the wind Clara was as good as finished. And, of course, I did think it over. I thought about it night and day, to the exclusion of everything else. . . ."

"No wonder the Crede people thought you were overtired!" Mollie said.

"Well, I tried to hide it, but it wasn't possible. I was in a state of mental agony. . . . Clara had always gone her own way, she'd insisted on living her own sort of life, she'd virtually told me to mind my own business when I'd reproached her about the kind of company she was keeping—but I still felt a deep sense of responsibility for her. I couldn't help thinking that at some stage

128

it must all have been my fault. And it wasn't only that. The most agonising thing to me was that Clara was exactly like her mother in appearance. The likeness haunted me. Every time I saw her it took me right back.... The thought of what might happen to her was torture. It was a sentimental feeling, I know, but I couldn't help it....

"Clara was pitifully frightened—and she had good reason to be. She swore to me that she hadn't visited Angel with the deliberate intention of killing him, but I felt she'd had the will to kill if she couldn't get her own way. The fact that she'd dropped the gun and rushed from the house in panic after the shooting was perhaps in her favour—though she'd obviously recovered her self-possession in a remarkably short time. I certainly didn't think she'd have the slightest chance with a jury, in view of the contents of that letter, and the fact that *two* shots had been fired, and that she'd made such calculated efforts to conceal her part in the affair afterwards. If I did nothing, it wasn't outside the bounds of possibility that she'd be hanged for a capital crime. At the very least, she'd spend the rest of her life in prison.... I couldn't face that. I couldn't abandon her. If she'd continued to be hard and brazen it might have been different, but she seemed full of genuine remorse about all that had happened. She swore she'd change her way of life, that she'd learned her lesson. She beseeched me to help her. There were some appalling scenes.... I don't expect anyone who hasn't been in my situation to approve of what I did—but to me it seemed I had no choice. She was a terrified child—my child. I knew I'd got to help her. I'd got to think of *some* way of satisfying Barr and lifting the threat from her...."

His voice had become unsteady as he relived his ordeal. For a moment or two we sat in silence as he struggled to recover his composure. It was impossible not to be moved by his story. Only Barr seemed completely unconcerned. He was toying with the knife, testing the point against the ball of his thumb, thoughtfully rather than demonstratively. I wondered uneasily if he *had* shot his bolt, after all.

Presently Landon took up his story once more. "Well," he said,

"I thought of everything. I even thought of killing Barr. I'd have done it without compunction if it would have helped. But he'd taken precautions against that—or said he had. He'd made a parcel of the gun and letter, he told me, with an accompanying note, and left it with Scotland Yard's address on it in a place where it would be found if anything happened to him. It may have been a bluff, but I couldn't risk it. . . ."

"It wasn't a bluff," Barr said.

"So I had to find some other way," Landon went on, ignoring him. "I had to turn my unique knowledge into cash and buy back Barr's evidence. Once the gun and letter were in my hands, I knew the police could never *prove* anything against Clara, and that meant that Barr would have lost his hold over us. The problem was, how to raise the money. I applied myself to it with the same concentration as though it had been a piece of vital research at Crede. The exceptional position I was in suggested the exceptional step. I doubted if my knowledge was marketable in any foreign country, even if I'd been prepared to sell it—but I knew that it was of the utmost value to my own country. Thinking along these lines gave me the idea. If I could fake my own kidnapping, I might be able to collect a ransom. I had no expectation that the Government would pay it, but I thought there was a very good chance that someone else might. . . . Anyhow, I decided to try—and once I'd made up my mind I spared no effort to produce a perfect plan."

"It was entirely your plan, was it?" I asked.

"Yes, it was my plan. I had to have Barr's physical co-operation, but I did all the working out myself."

"Was it you who chose this hiding place?"

"Yes. . . . In my rock-climbing days I'd done quite a lot of potholing, and this was one of the pots I'd explored. I described it and its location to Barr, and he and Clara came up here and secretly looked over it. Clara hated being underground, but she forced herself to do what was necessary. She showed more courage in the end than I'd have expected. . . . Anyhow, they both agreed it was the perfect place. I couldn't take any actual part in the preparations myself, because the security people were with me wherever I went. Barr had to do all the buying and provisioning. I told him where he could get potholing equipment, and drew up a list for him, and he bought everything—tent and sleeping-bag and rugs, lamp and fire, ladder and rope and fuel—and a boiler-suit and helmet for himself because he was constantly in and out with the supplies."

"I'd have thought someone might have remembered afterwards that he'd done it," I said. "His picture was in the papers, too."

"We thought of that. He disguised himself a little when he made the purchases, so there'd be no risk of identification."

"I see. . . . And I suppose he brought all the stuff in at night?"

"Yes—there was no danger that anyone would see him. Actually, all the preparations went very smoothly, and by 13th March, which was the Sunday I'd chosen for my disappearance, everything was ready for me here. . . ."

At that moment there was an interruption. Barr, I saw, was scrambling to his feet. I sprang up, too, and Landon half rose—but it was a false alarm. Barr moved the paraffin fire a yard closer to us and sat down again. "Sorry!" he said. "I feel a kind of chill in the air!"

"Go on, Landon," I said.

"Well, the faking of the actual kidnapping was a simple matter. I'd prepared the ground a little by telling as many people as possible that I proposed to visit my daughter that Sunday evening, so there'd appear to be many channels by which the information could have reached the kidnappers. In the morning Barr went along with a tin of treacle and some brown paper and broke the pane of glass over the back door while Clara played the radio loudly. Afterwards he took the treacle away and got rid of it. It was Barr, of course, who made the bogus telephone call to Clara at six o'clock. Clara went off to the hospital, leaving the light on so that the security police would think everything was all right when they got there. Having to light up so early was a weakness, but we were working to a tight schedule and it was impossible to start any later or I'd have missed a vital train. When I arrived I let myself in with the key Clara had given me, just as I'd done the week before. My having a key could be considered a weakness, too, but it was unavoidable—and the police certainly suspected nothing. I walked straight through the house, wiped the back door knobs and back door key on my way, and left by the back garden."

"How did you get to the station?"

"Barr was waiting with his car at the end of the path. He drove me to St. Pancras and I just caught the 7.10 to Chinley Junction—that's a place about seven miles from here. . . ."

As Landon paused again, I couldn't help recalling what Lawson had said about the need to check up on Barr's movements that evening. He'd never done so, of course, because his theory had collapsed—and neither had anyone else, since Barr had been under no suspicion. I wondered if it would have made any difference. Probably Barr would have produced some plausible account of his activities anyway.

I switched my mind back to the 7.10 for Chinley Junction. "What about the risk of being remembered afterwards? Did you have some sort of disguise, too?"

"I'd changed my clothes in the car," Landon said. "Barr had brought along a hiking outfit—sports jacket, flannels, walking shoes, cloth cap, rucksack and stick. The effect was to alter my appearance completely, especially as I'd removed my glasses. I dozed in a corner seat with my head well down and no one took any notice of me. I got to Chinley at 11.30 and walked here. I found everything in order and—well, I took up residence."

"And it was you who wrote the ransom letters?"

"Yes—I prepared the first one in the morning. We'd got everything ready here. Barr had brought down a stack of old newspapers, and gum, and the necessary envelopes and paper, and a pair of surgical gloves."

"A little while ago," I said, "you mentioned fifty thousand pounds. What made you cut the figure down to thirty thousand?"

"Barr decided that £30,000 in five-pound notes was about the maximum weight we could deal with, because it had to be hauled up the cliff and carried quite a distance and then manhandled through the tunnel."

"I see. . . . What about posting that first letter?—you did that yourself, I suppose?"

"Yes, I walked into Sheffield that morning and put it in a suburban box. I'd decided I'd be quite safe because it was too soon for any photographs of me to have appeared. Then I came back here and settled down to live as comfortably as I could."

"It must have been frightful," Mollie said. She was very much on the job now, packing away the information we were getting.

"Actually, Miss Bourne, it wasn't as bad as you might think. Physically I'd got everything I needed. The way I look now gives a false impression—I didn't wash much, or shave, simply because I thought a rather wild appearance would fit the picture of a kidnapped man better when I finally left. I ate sparingly, because a little loss of weight would serve the same purpose—but I had all I needed."

"And I suppose you were able to go out at night?" Mollie said.

"Yes, every night I went up for fresh air and exercise on the moors."

I said, "Wasn't there a risk that some of the local potholers might come exploring here during the weekend? That would have wrecked everything."

"The possibility did cross my mind, but it was an outside chance and I didn't let it worry me. To tell you the truth, Curtis, I'd almost got beyond worrying. I'd committed myself, and I'd got to go through with it and hope for the best."

I nodded. "Well—then what happened?"

"The next thing was that on the Wednesday night Barr drove up here, bringing me newspapers and a report of the latest developments. He told me the Press were saying I'd never be released alive even if the ransom money were paid, because I'd be able to describe my kidnappers. I obviously had to do something about that, so I wrote my personal letter explaining why I *wouldn't* be able to describe them. Barr made a detour on his way back to London and posted it at Staines, just to confuse things. Then, on the Friday night, he came up again with news of the *Record's* offer, and we composed another letter, accepting the offer and stating our terms. Barr posted that one in Saffron Walden."

"You were taking quite a chance, weren't you—of a trap?"

"We had to accept some risk. We thought that if we insisted on Clara accompanying the money, that would be a sufficient safeguard against the police being brought to the meeting place."

"I realise that—but what about the numbers of the notes being kept? Didn't that possibility worry Barr?"

"We took precautions," Landon said. "I'd thought out all these things. . . . When Barr called at the *Record* office ostensibly about the danger to Clara, and accused the *Record* of planning a doublecross, and made a scene, he was able to check up on the situation—and he went away completely satisfied that no trickery was going to be attempted."

"So that was why he came. . . .!" The pieces were falling neatly into place now. "Incidentally, what about that telephone call to the *Record* that was supposed to come from one of the kidnappers . . .? I assume that was Barr, too?"

"Yes, that was Barr. We felt it was essential that one of the supposed kidnappers should actually be *heard* by some independent person, to prove they really existed and bolster up my story when I got out. For the same reason, it was arranged that Clara should say she'd been rung up several times by the kidnappers, too. . . . Don't imagine I take any pride in these details, Curtis—I don't. I'm only telling you them to give a complete picture."

"He's got a tidy mind," Barr said.

"So then what happened?" I asked. "Who collected the suitcase on Mam Tor?"

"I collected it."

"It must have been quite a job."

"It *was* a job—it was heavy, and it kept sticking on the way up. It was a job carrying it here, too, because I had a big coil of rope as well. But I managed."

"Those ribbed footmarks we noticed on the moor—were they yours?"

"Yes, they were mine."

"What about the message you sent down the cliff saying you would be released to join Clara next evening and asking where she was staying . . .? Presumably you needed her around—but why?"

"Having her here was an essential part of the exchange arrangements I'd made with Barr. . . . You see, although I could identify on my own the letter that Clara had written to Angel, only she could positively identify the gun she'd used. That meant she had to stay up for a second night, since it would have been too late to make the exchange on the first night. We'd already prepared you for a delay by pretending we'd need twenty-four hours to check that the notes weren't marked, so that was all right. But there had to be an excuse for Clara to stay—and the note I lowered down the cliff gave it to her."

"Yes, I see. . . . Actually, how were you going to manage the exchange—I should think it could have been a pretty tricky operation. Were you going to trust each other?"

"We certainly weren't! Barr and I had worked out all the details with the minutest care, so that both parties would be safeguarded and neither would have a chance to cheat the other."

"May we hear them?" Mollie said.

"Well, Clara was to arrive first, at a quarter to eight, and join me down here. Barr was to come at half-past eight, bringing with him the letter and the gun in a parcel. On arrival at the top of the cavern he was to draw up the ladder and lower the parcel on the rope. Clara and I were to inspect the contents and satisfy ourselves that they were in order. Barr would know that we would have to let him have the money then, because otherwise he could take the ladder away with him, and though I could probably have climbed the rock face to the other passage, Clara couldn't. So he was safe. Having satisfied ourselves, we were to send the suitcase up on the rope. Barr was then to lower the ladder. We could rely on him doing that because he knew that if I had to I could get out on my own. So both sides were covered."

"Very ingenious!" I said. "And what was going to happen after that?"

"Barr was to take the money to his car, which he'd have left not far away on the moors, and drive back to London, and hide the suitcase in the loft of his garage. Clara was to follow him out of here and go back to the hotel in Castleton and wait there for my arrival. Around ten I was to join her there, saying the kidnappers had released me, and telling the detailed story I'd prepared.... Afterwards, if all went well, Barr was to fade quietly out of Clara's life, and eventually go abroad."

"To South America," Barr said. "And what an attractive prospect it was!"

"Well," Landon said, "the plan went wrong, as you know, because you and Miss Bourne followed Clara and were led to the pothole by my footmarks"

"Something else went wrong, didn't it?" I said. "Oughtn't Clara to have been down here when I found you?"

Landon said quietly, "She *was* here."

I stared at him.

"She arrived here punctually at a quarter to eight.... She was a bit worried because of the disturbing incident with Miss Bourne on the drive up the previous day, but of course she'd no idea she'd been followed to the moor. We sat talking about things, and waiting for Barr. Then your magnesium flare suddenly went off, and you called out, and Clara recognised your voice.... It was a frightful shock."

I could well believe it!

"I had to cope quickly with the new situation. I sent Clara back up the ladder and told her to pull it up behind her and wait at the top. I took my shoes off and hid them in my sleeping-bag and put slippers on instead so there could be no question of my climbing out with you at once. I pushed the suitcase well down under the pile of stores so that it couldn't be seen—and I made myself look as dirty and dishevelled as possible...."

"It was quite an act," I said, regarding him wonderingly.

"I had to do it, Curtis. Once you start these things you have to go through with them—and I thought I could see a way out. I knew Barr should be approaching the pothole at that moment—we'd agreed to keep to a strict time schedule. If I could get you and your companion to go for the police, I reckoned that Barr should be safely inside the tunnel before you reached the exit, and you'd miss him. Then there would be time for the exchange to be made and for Clara and Barr to get clear away before you returned. I couldn't be certain things would go smoothly, but it was the only hope. First, though, I had to convince you that while I was anxious to leave with you by the way you'd come, I couldn't. I'm afraid that was another act. I gave the impression of being so weak, as well as shoeless, that you naturally wouldn't hear of it—and you went off to get help."

"He'd make a good scoutmaster!" Barr said.

"Up to a point, all went well," Landon continued. "Barr *was* already in the tunnel, and he joined us on time. I told him what had happened, and we quickly concocted a story he could tell in case he and Clara ran into your rescue party on their way out. Then we made the exchange according to plan. Barr lowered the parcel, and Clara identified the gun...."

I interrupted him. "The gun had been unloaded, I take it ...?"

"What do *you* think!" Barr said sardonically.

"Oh, yes," Landon said, "it was part of the safeguard plan that Barr should remove the undischarged cartridges before he brought it down.... When we were satisfied, we tied the suitcase to the rope and Barr hauled it up and lowered the ladder and started back along the tunnel. Clara went off after him. I burned the letter and hid the gun in a rock fissure behind my stores where no one would be likely to find it after my 'rescue.' I also found a safe hiding place for my shoes, because I'd told you the kidnappers had taken them away. I made sure that nothing whatever would be found that wasn't compatible with my having been genuinely kidnapped. Then I waited. If you hadn't come back into the tunnel, I think the plan would have succeeded after all.... By the way, why *didn't* you carry on and fetch the police?"

I told him about the missing boiler-suit and helmet. "Ah!—yes, I'm afraid I overlooked that.... Well, there it is—you know the rest.... There's just one other thing I'd like to say, though. I realise I've behaved in a way that must seem to you quite fantastic and wholly reprehensible—but each man answers to his own conscience, and mine won't trouble me. In the situation I was in, I'd do the same thing again. I don't believe that any father with any normal feelings would willingly risk having his daughter hanged for murder if there was anything he could do to prevent it. But that doesn't mean I had any illusions about Clara—or about what might have happened to her afterwards. I *hoped* that if we pulled off this tremendous gamble, she might be able to salvage some sort of a life for herself from the wreckage. But I always doubted it. It's quite possible she did intend to kill Angel. I don't think she could ever have been really happy again. I think it's better that I failed, and that she died. . . "

Chapter Nineteen

There was a heavy silence after he'd finished. It was, indeed, a fantastic story—a story so removed from ordinary experience that any kind of judgment seemed irrelevant. Genius, they said, was akin to madness—and Landon's behaviour, if not mad, had certainly been wildly abnormal. Happily, we didn't have to pass any judgment. For Mollie and me, the only thing that mattered now—apart from making sure that Barr got his deserts—was to get out of this cavern alive and find a telephone and put over what was undoubtedly going to be a sensational front-page splash.

When and whether we'd be able to do that seemed, at the moment, distinctly moot. Barr, with a prospective prison sentence stretching ahead of him to infinity, obviously wasn't going to let any of us go free to tell the news if he could help it—and that ugly-looking knife still gave him the edge on us. A concerted rush by Landon and myself would probably overpower him, but that knife could kill, and Barr had already shown himself a potential killer. Rushing on cold steel in cold blood wasn't exactly a beckoning prospect.

At the same time, Barr himself was in a pretty weak position. If he forced the issue by attacking us, one of us would be sure to get him. If he didn't, he looked like being here for a long while. With the tunnel blocked, and the other passage approachable only up a rock face that he hadn't the skill to climb, he had no way of escape. Even when the tunnel was clear he'd never be able to go up that ladder as long as we were free to swing it from below. We seemed to have reached a deadlock and I couldn't see how it was going to be broken—unless Barr did something rash. That was the danger.

Mollie tried reasoning with him. She said quietly, "You know, Barr, you might just as well give up—you haven't a hope of getting away with this. You can't possibly deal with us all—and sooner or later we're going to be found here. Three people have disappeared from Castleton—and your car's out there on the moor to show a search party where to start looking. It's merely a question of time. And if you've used that knife when we're found, you'll only get a heavier sentence still."

It was a good effort—but not good enough. The fact was that even if a search party thought of potholes, the whole district was studded with them and it might take weeks for the searchers to find us. Still, I backed her up, as forcefully as I could. "She's right, Barr," I said, "you haven't a chance. You can't get away. If you start anything, you're bound to get hurt. You'd be much wiser to hand over that knife and call it a day."

He grinned. "If you two feel like going on talking" he said, "do by all means. . . . Personally I intend to have something to eat."

He got up, with the knife defensively poised, and backed away to Landon's food store behind the tent. I couldn't see him very well, but I could hear the rustle of paper. I looked around—perhaps while he was out of the way I could find some weapon. . . . But everything useful was behind the tent. There was an uneasy silence, broken only by the faint hiss of the pressure stove. I wondered what the stove would be like as a weapon. I lifted it experimentally. It was very unwieldy—certainly no match for a knife. It seemed to be going out, and I started to pump it. The container must have been empty, for with a final hiss the flame died. I was just going to ask Landon where the fuel was when I heard a fresh sound—a faint click that stirred old memories. I sprang up in alarm.

"The gun!" I cried. "Landon, I believe he's found the gun!"

"It's not loaded," Landon said. "I looked—it was empty."

"It's *being* loaded . . .! Quick!" I took a step towards the tent—but I was too late. At that moment Barr came out from behind it, pointing the gun. He must have had the unused bullets in his pocket all the time. I turned and took a flying kick at the paraffin lamp. It went up into the air and dropped with a crash and the light went out. At once the darkness in the cave was blacker than night. I grabbed Mollie and pulled her down to the floor and we retreated on hands and knees out of the alcove and into the main cavern. Over on my right, I could hear Landon working his way back, too. Presently we stopped to listen. Barr was still in the alcove. He seemed to be searching among the stores again.

I called out, "Landon!—how many bullets does the chamber hold?"

"Five." His voice, calm and steady, came from some yards away to the right.

I thought quickly. It wasn't likely that Barr would have had any bullets with him except those he'd taken out of the gun. Two had been fired. That still left him with one for each of us—but it meant he couldn't afford to waste one. He'd have to come close and make sure of his aim before he fired. That might give us a chance.

Suddenly a light flickered on. Somewhere in that dump of equipment Barr had found a torch. That altered things again. It wasn't a very bright light, but with the gun it gave him complete control of the situation. He was flashing it around the alcove. Presently he came out. He was moving very cautiously—we could be anywhere in that vast place, and he'd lost track of us. He began to work his way to and fro across the cavern, shining the light all round him, making sure that his rear and flanks were safe. As he criss-crossed, he slowly advanced.

My spirits sank. I didn't see how he could fail to hunt us down in the end if he kept going. But it would take time. There were too many obstructions in his path, too many places of concealment for us—particularly at the sides of the cave, where the stalagmite grew like a forest. We continued our retreat, over the shallow stream and back across the open floor towards the rock face where I'd climbed down. I couldn't hear Landon any more. I hoped he wasn't trying to slip by behind Barr, or he'd surely be found.

If only I had some weapon! I kicked hard at a piece of stalagmite and it snapped off. It was about an inch in diameter and a foot long, with a fairly sharp point. It was very light and brittle, but better than nothing. I gave it to Mollie, and broke another piece off for myself.

Mollie whispered urgently, "What's the plan?"

I said, "Pray that he misses!"

We continued to go back. There wasn't much farther we *could* go now. But at least we were deep among the stalagmite, and it would give us some cover, as well as slowing Barr.

I looked cautiously out. Barr was still criss-crossing the floor. He was out now in the emptiest part of the cavern—the least obstructed, and the widest. Suddenly there was a noise on his left. He swung the torch. It was Landon, doubling back close to the wall, trying to take him in the rear. There was a flash, and an ear-splitting report. Landon gave a ghastly yell, staggered out into the open, dropped to his knees, rolled over once, and lay still. It had all happened so fast I hadn't even had time to move.

Barr took a perfunctory look at the crumpled remains of Landon. Then the little pool of light began to advance again. He'd *got* to finish us now—for what he'd done, he'd hang, anyway. Massacre was his only hope. I reached out and found Mollie's hand. "I guess this is it," I said softly. "I'll try and rush him when he gets close. Join in if you get the chance." I felt the pressure of her hand in return. It was like a farewell. I peered again through the stalagmite rods. Barr was coming on in a slightly crouching position. He must know he had us cornered. I couldn't see a ray of hope.

Then, suddenly, I froze. The corpse of Landon was moving. Not just showing signs of life, but moving like a man unhurt, on all fours, on hands and silent, stockinged feet, up behind Barr. He'd only been shamming dead! Hope surged back. We still had a chance—and it was now or never. I sprang up and rushed into the open cave, weaving and zigzagging. Barr saw me, fired at me, and missed. I kept going, shouting like a maniac to drown any sound from behind him. Landon was almost there. He *was* there. He was on Barr's back like a panther, trying to drag him down. But he hadn't the weight or the strength. Barr flung him off and cracked the butt of the gun on his head as he fell. As he steadied himself to fire at me again I hurled my piece of stalagmite in his face and

142

dived for his legs. He went over with a crash as I sprawled into him—but he still had the gun. I scrambled on top of him, fighting to hold his wrist down. He was bashing at me savagely with his free hand. He was immensely strong. The hand with the gun began to come up. I was concentrating so hard on the gun I couldn't guard my face. I *had* to keep the gun down. Then Mollie was there, primitive as they come, jabbing the sharp end of her stalagmite rod into his arm with all her strength. He gave a yell of pain and his fingers loosed their grip on the gun. Mollie grabbed it. Now I had two hands free and things were different. I struggled up and so did Barr. His face was distorted with rage in the faint torch glow. He lashed out wildly and missed me. For a second that rugged chin of his stuck out just a shade too far. I gathered all my weight and hit it fair and square on the point and followed through. He crashed down among the limestone debris and didn't move again.

I gasped, "Thanks, Mollie!" and picked up the torch. She was already bending over Landon. He was sitting up, holding his head, but he wasn't seriously damaged. By a miracle, we'd all come through alive. That brilliant sham—his last act, and his best—had saved us.

Chapter Twenty

We lashed Barr up with the rope when he came round and he didn't give any further trouble. Mollie ministered to our minor injuries very competently—next to starting a fight, there was nothing she could do better than tend the wounded! We spent most of the night in the cavern—I didn't feel like scaling the rock face again, and it was after five before the tunnel was sufficiently free of water for me to get through. Then I went down to the road and rang for help. By seven o'clock the moor was so crowded with policemen it looked as though they were on manœuvres. By nine, they'd got everyone out of the pothole, and we were all driven off to the local station to make statements. Barr and Landon were naturally kept there. I felt sorry for Landon, on many counts, but of course there could be no simple way out for him. He'd have to face the music, and it was going to be quite an orchestra. All the same, I had a feeling the judge would make all possible allowances for him when the time came, and that meanwhile he'd be working his passage home, back on the job at Crede. Whatever he'd done, he was too valuable a man to waste.

A few of the police stayed behind at the pothole to search for Clara's body. Others took charge of the thirty thousand pounds. Mollie and I were finally allowed to go back to the hotel. I rang Grant and gave him an account of the tremendous happenings, and Mollie rang the *Courier*. Then we both went to work on our stories. By the time we'd phoned them, the first London reporters were beginning to arrive in Castleton and we decided to slip away before they started to take us apart. I'd have liked to drive Mollie back in the Riley, but she said the hire people would be wanting the Zephyr. I went out into the drive with her. As I closed the door of her car she leaned out, smiling.

"Well—it was quite a hunch, wasn't it?"

"It was, wonder girl!"

"I couldn't have done anything without you, though."

I gave an ironical bow. "Very generous of you!" I said.

"Honestly, Hugh, I thought you were marvellous."

"Good! Just try and hold that!"

She laughed. "What are you going to do when you get back to town?"

"Have a good sleep," I said.

"So am I—but afterwards?"

"What do you suggest?"

"If you cared to come round to the flat about nine I could make you some coffee."

I said, "This is where I came in. . . . What about those chances you'd be taking?"

She gave me a charming smile. "This time," she said, "perhaps I'll *really* be in the mood!"

THE END

www.ingramcontent.com/pod-product-compliance
Ingram Content Group UK Ltd.
Pitfield, Milton Keynes, MK11 3LW, UK
UKHW040105010325
455690UK00002B/18